Ally ~~grew up on a farm~~ rm
near ~~...~~ s for
children and teens. Her books have been nominated
for and won numerous awards. Before becoming an
author, she had many jobs including working as an
archaeologist, a classroom helper, a museum guard,
a giant teddy bear and a singer and songwriter.

Ally lives in Somerset with her husband and four
children.

Praise for Ally Kennen

"A thrilling and original adventure"
Guardian

"A pitch-perfect blend of humour, adventure and emotion"
Sunday Telegraph

"Funny, entertaining and surprisingly moving and it is this …
that lifts the book above the ordinary"
Philip Ardagh, *Guardian*

"*Sparks* has a beautiful emotional intelligence and humour that
make its suspense all the more enjoyable. It is one of the best
new books for 9+ out this year"
The Times

"Enterprising writing of a high calibre"
Independent on Sunday

"Proof that magic is really all around us"
Guardian

CUMBRIA LIBRARIES

3 8003 04766 4099

KT-491-335

"Ally Kennen began her writing career well with an acclaimed book for teens and has gone from strength to strength with each subsequent novel… Well-observed, witty and moving"
Sunday Times

"Ally Kennen is a wonderful storyteller and she draws the reader in to this novel with its excellent characterisation and bittersweet plot"
Scotsman

"Inventive, funny and moving family adventure …
one of the season's stand-outs"
Children's Bookseller – Ones to Watch

"Refreshingly different … a well written tale with much wisdom embedded in the telling. Words that are inspiring, challenging and encouraging convey the message that the beloved dead are always with us to inspire, challenge, encourage"
School Librarian

"Rings with talent and compelling detail …
a tense, funny and touching tale"
Amanda Craig, *The Times*

"An extraordinary imaginative achievement … this is a compassionate story from an exciting new voice"
Bookseller

ALLY KENNEN

THE EVERYTHING MACHINE

SCHOLASTIC

Scholastic Children's Books
An imprint of Scholastic Ltd
Euston House, 24 Eversholt Street, London, NW1 1DB, UK
Registered office: Westfield Road, Southam, Warwickshire, CV47 0RA
SCHOLASTIC and associated logos are trademarks and/or
registered trademarks of Scholastic Inc.

First published in the UK by Scholastic Ltd, 2017

Text copyright © Ally Kennen, 2017

The right of Ally Kennen to be identified as the author
of this work has been asserted by her.

ISBN 978 1407 13855 8

A CIP catalogue record for this book
is available from the British Library.

All rights reserved.
This book is sold subject to the condition that it shall not, by
way of trade or otherwise, be lent, hired out or otherwise circulated in
any form of binding or cover other than that in which it is published. No
part of this publication may be reproduced, stored in a retrieval system,
or transmitted in any form or by any means (electronic, mechanical,
photocopying, recording or otherwise) without prior
written permission of Scholastic Limited.

Printed by CPI Group (UK) Ltd, Croydon, CR0 4YY
Papers used by Scholastic Children's Books are made
from wood grown in sustainable forests.

1 3 5 7 9 10 8 6 4 2

This is a work of fiction. Names, characters, places, incidents
and dialogues are products of the author's imagination or are used
fictitiously. Any resemblance to actual people, living or dead,
events or locales is entirely coincidental.

www.scholastic.co.uk

Contents

For Thomas Ralph

Thanks to Dan Amos for his help with the
"thought-leak" code and the inspiration
behind two forward slashes saving the
world... //

chapters[1].title =
"The Wrong Delivery";

Mum was out when the delivery men came. She'd popped down to the shops with the baby for some Frizzy Fries and Mongoose Cake. I was at home because I'd been to the dentist that afternoon and I'd had to have a filling. One side of my face was still numb and I kept drooling like a mad dog.

To cheer myself up I was playing MAZZO on my phone. It's this incredible game about surviving on Mars and you have to blast the hideous Orsps and protect the Mars Queen. I play it every day. Everyone does. Even teachers. Even the ancient teachers who talk longingly about the days when their ancestors were allowed to hit children with sticks.

And when the doorbell exploded (my sister, Bird, has rewired it so that it sounds like our house is being blasted to bits whenever anyone presses it), our dog, Piggy, went into a mad frenzy of barking and I answered it, thinking Bird or Stevie had lost their keys.

But instead there was this huge, bald, sweaty-looking bloke in a blue boiler suit, holding a clipboard. Behind him was a dirty white van with another bloke sitting inside, munching on a chocolate bar.

"Delivery for a Mr O Fugue?" the man said, handing me a pen. I nodded, my stomach giving a roll of excitement. I'd been expecting this.

I signed the bit of paper with my latest signature, with an enormous "O" for Olly. I thought it looked like a famous footballer's signature. I intend to be a famous footballer when I grow up and this signature might be worth something one day.

"Where do you want us to put it? It's blimmin' heavy," said the bloke. He had a strong Birmingham accent, which is not surprising because that's where we live. Our bit of the city is between two hectic roads, the M54, which goes to Wales, where my mum's from, and the M5, which goes to Devon, where everyone goes camping in the rain.

"Wound the back, pwease," I slurred through my swollen mouth.

The bloke nodded, climbed back into the van, and reversed it up the short driveway round the side of our house.

Our house is in a street with lots of other houses just like it. The best thing about it is the long, long garden which is five times as big as everyone else's. The worst thing about our house is that it is painted pink, like an antique rose, says Mum. Like an ancient, warped PC drive monitor, says Bird. Like the pink shirts of Scotland FC 2016 away shirts, say I. Like my bum, says Stevie. (He is my little brother.)

I unlocked the gate, holding tightly to Piggy's collar, and watched as the two men unloaded an enormous crate.

They slid it on a ramp and then on to a trolley thing.

"I'm not gonna do my back in!" the first one said. "I'm off on holiday tonight. I'm flying to Spain!" He smiled a smile of pure sunshine.

"And I'm off to Malta," said the second, who had a neatly clipped beard and was wearing an Arsenal shirt. "Get me tan topped up, innit. Holiday of a lifetime."

I directed them down the garden path, past the swing and to MY mobile home.

I say MY mobile home, because it is MINE, apart from my sister's solar panels on the roof. It was here before we'd even moved in and it is gigantic, about the size of two buses glued together. Mum has got roses growing all over it, even the roof. We call it the "Mob" and no one comes in without my permission. (Apart from Stevie because it is HIS as well.) It's busy in there, with old skateboards and bits of bicycles and the world's smallest football pitch.

Dad took out most of the internal walls so there is one big room and a tiny bedroom and loo at the back. (The loo is NOT to be used under any circumstances as it is not plumbed in any more, but I've got a sunflower-from-school growing/dying in it.)

I was worried that the crate wouldn't fit through the door, but with quite a lot of rude words (some of them were brand new to me), the men managed it.

"What've you got in here, anyway?" asked the sweaty bloke, who was now sweating so much it looked like his forehead was crying. "It weighs a blinking tonne."

I wrinkled my nose, which is what I do when I am feeling shy.

"It's a hutch for my pets," I slurred.

"What pets?" asked the Arsenal-shirt bloke. "A rhinoceros?" He shot a look at Piggy, who is a small, brown, scruffy terrier with black paws and a restless personality.

"Wabbits," I replied, wiping spit from my chin.

By now we were all crowded inside. I'd quickly shoved my stuff to the sides and heaved the big old armchair out of the way.

Sweaty man looked round. "How many rabbits have you got?" he asked. "I can't see any."

The truth was I had no rabbits. But I'd figured that if I got a hutch, then the rabbits would follow. And this hutch had cost three pounds and fifty-six pence. I'd used Dad's eBay account. The whole family know his password. (It's P.A.S.S.W.O.R.D.)

"Ouch," said Sweaty, holding his arm. "Brutal nail there."

A nail jutted out of the door. It's where Dad used to hang his spare house key. Dad doesn't need it any more because he left us two months ago.

"I think you'll all be happier without me," he said just before he left, playing with the strap of his battered leather bag.

He was wrong. We are not happy without him. Even though he had been as grumpy as a hungry lion and arguing with Mum since he lost his job, we still miss him.

A lot.

He has only phoned four times. We don't know where he is staying. He said soon he would have his own place and we could come over and see him but that hasn't happened yet.

Anyway, how did I get on to Dad?

"I haven't got any Wabbits," I admitted in a spitty voice.

The men looked at each other as if to say, "We've got a right one here."

"OK," said Sweaty. "We're off." He looked at me. "Where's your mum, anyway?"

"Gone to gwet milk," I said. (For she had not really gone to get Frizzy Fries and Mongoose cake, I just said that to make things more interesting).

"What's that?" asked Arsenal-shirt, looking at my sister's home-made wind generator at the end of the garden. It's about four metres high and made almost entirely from plastic milk bottles.

"School pwroject," I said. If you say "school project" to grown-ups they usually leave you alone.

"And what are these plants? They look like something out of MAZZO." Arsenal waved at the giant rhubarb growing all along the back fence. The stuff towers over us and has leaves as big as tractor wheels.

"Mum planted a wittle piece two years ago but it has taken over..."

"Cheers, mate," said Sweaty, not really listening. "Job done." He and Arsenal hi-fived.

And then they were off, back up the path and out to their van.

They drove away in a puff of bad-smelling smoke, leaving a chocolate wrapper twisting in the gutter.

Me and Piggy ran into the Mob and bolted the door behind us.

My Mob has a long, low table at one end and rows of shelves fixed to the walls. I've got all my dad's dusty tools hanging on hooks on the back wall. Dad used to like making bits and bobs like bird feeders and benches but he went off it. Mum doesn't come in here. She hasn't been in for ages. She says it reminds her of Dad and she is happy to leave it all to me (and Stevie), which suits us just fine.

I selected a screwdriver from its hook and carefully unscrewed one corner of the crate. There were ten screws along the top and five down each side.

When I'd finished, I carefully edged the panel away from the frame and walked it back to the wall. I propped it up and wriggled out. Then I looked inside the crate and read a label.

DEADLY. DO NOT TAMPER
WITH CONTENTS.

I sucked in my breath. Piggy looked at me and I looked at Piggy.

This was no rabbit hutch.

I'd been sent the wrong thing.

Very, very, very wrong.

```
chapters[2].title =
```

"The DEADLY Machine";

I was looking at a machine, about the size of two large fridge-freezers, wrapped tight with clear plastic.

I told myself I was not going to *tamper* with it, just *look* at it.

Selecting scissors from the row of tools, I cut a slit along the top of the plastic. The machine smelled of oil and rubber and plastic and metal.

Then I got the heebie-jeebies, thinking *DEADLY, DEADLY, DEADLY.* I checked out of the window. All clear, but Sweaty and Arsenal were bound to return, once they'd realized their mistake. In the meantime, there'd be no harm in investigating (not tampering) just a bit more.

I found a pouch with folded paper inside.

RUSSELL: 1,000,000 PROTOTYPE.
PROPERTY OF NASA & MOD & BSA
& ROSCOSMOS & NATO & GRU

Russell? What kind of a name was that? Why would anyone call a machine "Russell"?

I knew NASA was the American Space Agency and MOD stood for the Ministry of Defence. So this Russell-thingy belonged to the army and people like that.

"Prototype", I believed, meant the first of its kind.

So what the heck did RUSSELL do?

The machine was nearly as tall as me and was made of metal and white plastic and had a big, flat space at the bottom and an arm-thing reaching down, like the wood-working machines you get in factories and school carpentry workshops.

There were five round hoppers, or capsules, set into the top, each one having a different-coloured lid. A wide computer screen flickered faintly on the front, which was weird because it wasn't plugged in

I turned the piece of paper over and read.

PIONEERING 3D PRINTING TECHNOLOGY.

Well, well, I thought, doesn't a pioneer have something to do with squirrels?

So did this machine *print squirrels?* That wasn't DEADLY.

Maybe "pioneer" meant something else. If I were Bird, my sister, I'd go and look it up in the dictionary. But I'm not that sort. I'm more of a guesser.

I knew only vaguely what a 3D printer was. Instead of printing words or pictures on a page, it could print THINGS. So what could I print with this? I might as well have some fun with it before NASA, or whoever had had a rabbit hutch delivered to them, worked out something had gone wrong and came to pick it up. My eye fell on an instruction leaflet.

This is RUSSELL 1,000,000. The most cutting-edge technology IN THE WORLD.

With the right ingredients this machine can make pretty much ANYTHING – guitars, plastic models, meat, any engine parts, complex computers, weapons or synthetic skin! The last time this machine was tested it printed a WORKING TRACTOR! With Russell, the sky really isn't the limit (because you could make an aeroplane should you wish).

I rubbed my hands together, excitement fizzing through me. None of this sounded DEADLY.

I could print a car or a house. I could print medals, a lawnmower, a guitar. I could print FOOD. I could print toys and games and really anything I wanted. But what should I print out first?

I couldn't wait to get started.

I was flicking through the booklet, having wilder and wilder ideas, when I heard the back gate slam and feet pattering down the path.

The door rattled against the bolt and Piggy wagged his tail.

"Olly. It's me. Let me in. What are you up to in there?"

My brother had come back from school.

"Just give me a minute." I quickly propped the wooden lid against the machine. Should I let Stevie in on this? He's nine, two years younger than me, and if I wasn't careful, he might tell Mum. He's a good kid but he's a talker.

So I decided to keep it to myself. This was MY thing, at least until the owners came.

I left the door bolted.

Then the window burst open and Stevie poked his head through.

"What in the name of heck is that?"

```
chapters[3].title =
```
"The Instructions";

"It's just … a wabbit hutch," I said, in a lame attempt to preserve my secret.

"NO, IT IS NOT. I CAN READ, DUMB-BUM. IT'S A 3D PRINTING MACHINE!" squealed Stevie, who had climbed in through the window and was already poking and prodding and fiddling with Russell. "OH, MY GOD! This is the most EXCITING thing that has EVER HAPPENED TO ME."

"Actually, this thing is happwening to me, wot you," I said. "It's got my wame on it."

But Stevie wasn't listening.

"We can make anything. ANYTHING," he yelled,

waving the instructions like a team flag at a match. His eyes glinted with a flash of evil.

"We could build an army of fighting robots and take over the town!"

"Why would you want to do that?" I asked.

"No more school," replied Stevie. "I could become KING. And, anyway, why are you talking funny?"

"Dentist. You'd just be a weevil leader and everyone would hate you."

"OK," replied Stevie. "How about we build an army of robots anyway? We don't have to take over the town. But we could make them fight each other and it would be fun!"

"We should start with something simple," I said firmly. "Start at the bottom and work our way up."

"NO WAY," replied Stevie, pulling the rest of the wood off with a jackhammer. "We should start with something complicated and learn from our mistakes."

It seemed that I was no longer on my own in this project. I worked my mouth around. The feeling was finally coming back after the dentist's injection.

"Let's make another Stinky Elephant," said Stevie. "My old pal could have a brother."

Stinky Elephant was Stevie's Stinky Elephant. He'd had him since birth and he loved him very deeply, probably more than he loved the rest of us. Our dog, Piggy, viewed Stinky Elephant as a deadly enemy and had a sneaky chew on him whenever he could. We were all terrified Stevie would lose the thing and mourn for ever. Stevie loved elephants. He said he was going to work in a zoo when he grew up and ride them every day.

"Maybe I won't make another one," said Stevie. "Stinky might get jealous."

I scratched my head and looked at the machine in front of me. I did want to MAKE something, but what, what, what?

"How about a football?" Hurrah! I could speak normally again.

Stevie looked deflated.

"Olly, we can make anything in the world and you want to make a football? You don't need a machine for that, you just need a fiver, for crikey's sake."

I looked round the room for inspiration.

What thing did I want most in the world, apart from rabbits? I couldn't think. I'd had lots of Lego for Christmas and I already had a bike.

"I know," said Stevie. "Make me a Space Hound."

You remember I told you about MAZZO? The coolest game ever? I play it on my phone. Stevie plays it on Mum's tablet and Bird plays it on her Headsetz. Anyway, so we're all on MARS, trying to survive in the hostile environment, but the best things are the Space Hounds, which have been bred to survive on Mars. They are very friendly, fluffy, HUGE dogs and the Queen has a whole pack of them to protect her. In MAZZO, Stevie has the important job of Kennel Master. He helps looks after the Queen's Space Hounds.

"A REAL little Space Hound, to take to school and be my friend," said Stevie pleadingly.

"You've got lots of friends," I said. My brother was Mr Popular Pants. I'm obviously not jealous. I am just more select in my choice of friends. Very select indeed. I am so choosy about friends, I only really have one,

Raz, who has size eight feet, can burp in French and is a very strong defender.

"Pleeeaseee, Ollleeeee." Stevie blinked at me and smiled. He was wearing his MAZZO T-shirt with a picture of a Space Hound on it. The caption read *"COSMIC CANINES RULE"*.

Stevie owns MAZZO pants, MAZZO pyjamas, a MAZZO lunchbox and MAZZO pencils. He had MAZZO trainers and socks and a MAZZO rucksack. He makes Mum read him official MAZZO stories at night. Even Stinky Elephant wears a mini MAZZO jumper. The boy is completely obsessed with MAZZO and he would play it all day if he were allowed, which he isn't. The light was fading, so we switched on the table lamp, though it didn't make much difference, and unpacked the rest of the machine, folding away the plastic and unwrapping lots of little bits of equipment. Then we started to put the thing together. The instructions were weird, like a series of mad crossword clues. But we battled through them, like rats in a maze.

Eventually we plugged the whole machine in and switched it on at the wall.

I pressed the red button and the machine started humming.

I looked anxiously at the door. Would Mum hear? It sounded almost tuneful, like our old boiler singing.

Then we heard a deep, cheerful voice coming out of the speaker and I was so surprised I nearly weed myself.

"YOU GOT THERE! CONGRATULATIONS. NOW WE CAN GET GOING!"

```
chapters[4].title =
```

"MAZZO";

The machine spoke to us! It had a voice like a wacky headmaster all fired up on a Monday morning.

"HELLO. MY NAME IS RUSSELL. WHAT ARE YOUR NAMES?"

"Hi," I said cautiously. "I'm Olly and this is Stevie."

"EXCELLENT. HI, OLLY AND STEVIE."

"Russell?" said Stevie, creeping closer. "Why Russell?"

"THE MAN WHO DESIGNED ME THOUGHT IT WAS FUNNY TO NAME ME RUSSELL."

Then we heard Mum calling us in for dinner.

"Oh, rat snot," I said.

"What do we tell Russell?" whispered Stevie.

"We don't need to tell him anything, he's just a machine."

I shut the door very carefully.

In the kitchen, Mum was jiggling Ella, our baby sister, on her hip and doling out peas. Mum is quite a small person, but can be very loud. Her long, blonde hair was twisted into a plait thing on her head. She had a smear of baby slime on the shoulder of her grey dress. Granny's ruby earrings (a magnet for the baby) glowed in her ears.

Bird was sitting on the kitchen sofa, wearing her Headsetz and playing MAZZO. Stevie immediately went to look in the teeny tiny screen just above Bird's ear, which showed the outside world what Bird was seeing.

"So what have you two been up to out there?" asked Mum.

"School project," I replied.

"Bird, turn that thing off," said Mum. "Come and eat with us. Be human."

"Process nearly complete," murmured Bird, from

under her Headsetz. "Just got to save a thousand citizens from a raging Orsp invasion."

In MAZZO, Orsps come up from the ground and you have to shove them back in their holes or blast them, otherwise they all fold round you and steal your oxygen and dognap your Space Hounds. Orsps are as thin as paper and their eyes are like rips.

"Do you want to borrow a lob-bomb?" asked Stevie. "I've got loads."

"TURN IT OFF NOW," snapped Mum.

"Wait," said Bird. "I am an Elite Martian Scientist. I protect my people. That's why they voted me into the Futures Project."

"Has she gone utterly insane?" Mum turned to me. "What is she talking about? When I was little, I spoke to my parents like this. 'Billy Smith tried to trip me up. Frances ate his bogeys in assembly. When can I get some roller skates?' There was none of this 'Futures Project' business or blasting of Orbs."

"Not Orbs, Orsps," said Bird, whipping off her Headsetz, which had left track marks on her forehead. "Saved! I have a hundred per cent record of good people-care. Not bad for an Elite Scientist. What's for dinner? It smells horrible."

"Steak pie, carrots and peas," said Mum.

"Yuk. I prefer Martian food," said Bird. "Honey pods and raccoon juice."

"Me too," said Stevie. "I like rock chips and frozen jelly."

Carefully nudging Stevie's Stinky Elephant aside, Bird sat next to me. She's fourteen years old but she's only as tall as me. Don't let that fool you into thinking she's some kind of softie. She's not. She has powers. She knows how to fix the internet, debug computers, build crazy websites and put up firewalls. She's got this very cool sideways haircut and seems to know about everything before it happens. Like baby Ella. When Mum and Dad sat us down and announced they were having another baby, Bird had already told us six weeks earlier.

"So the hutch came then," she said.

How does she know? How, how, how?

"Sort of," I replied cautiously.

"OH, OLIVER," said Mum, passing me a plate of

steaming pie. "Why do you want rabbits so much? Why not another dog or a cat?"

Sleeping in his basket, Piggy raised a crooked ear at the word "cat".

"Dogs stare at you all the time," I said. "They're like stalker-fans."

"Agreed," said Bird. "If dogs were on Facebook they'd 'like' everything that ever was and take down the network. Complete over-sharers."

"And cats are furry demons with a bad agenda," I went on. "But rabbits are simple. Cuddly, big ears, not too demanding."

"Sounds like you are describing yourself," said Bird, pouring out glasses of water for everyone.

Mum leaned over and ruffled my hair. "Sorry," she said. "But rabbits breed and breed and we'd get overrun."

"Like you are with children," said Bird.

Mum coughed on a forkful of pie and baby Ella banged her on the forehead with a spoon.

"SSSSS, Gas-min."

The only words my baby sister can sort of say are "Shhh" and "Jasmine", which is Mum's name.

She's only about eleven months old so I think this is normal.

"Get two boy rabbits then," persisted Stevie.

"Rabbits are sneaky," said Mum. "Sometimes they just pretend to be boys."

"You could get them reviewed by a vet," suggested Bird. "An expert who would see through any pretending."

"All vets have off days," said Mum.

I fell silent. I was playing the long game. One day I would get some rabbits. Time and persistence would wear the woman down.

"Olly, I *need* to play MAZZO after tea," said Stevie apologetically. "It's really, really, really important. The Queen pinged me. One of the Space Hounds is ill."

Mum groaned. "None of this is REAL."

"It is to us," said Stevie. This was just like Stevie. He loved MAZZO so much he'd rather play it than investigate the amazing talking machine in the Mob.

"But what about our thingy?" I said.

"What thingy?" asked Bird. "What's more important than the Mars Queen pinging him?"

"Just a boy thing," I said.

"I like boy things," said Bird. "Even though *all* boy things are girl things too."

"Not *all* boy things," I said. "You can't wee *up*."

"Who says?" said Bird.

After that we got swept up in the MAZZO playing session. Mum would have been suspicious if we hadn't played.

I'd found an Orsp field and I get twenty oxygen points every time I blast one. Stevie has a more important job than me. As a Kennel Master, he has to feed all the Space Hounds every day, look after Space Puppies and stop them getting stolen by Orsps. Mum has a timer which buzzes when our MAZZO hour is over. Of course, sometimes we reset the timer when she isn't looking, so we get extra MAZZO minutes, but tonight she had the buzzer with her, so when it went off we had to stop.

"PLEASE! I BEG YOU TO LET ME PLAY A BIT MORE," pleaded Stevie. "The palace is surrounded by Orsps. I need to blast them before they steal the Space Hounds."

"No," said Mum, who was feeding the baby and reading her book.

"BUT IT'S IMPORTANT! THE QUEEN DEPENDS ON ME!"

"No," said Mum, looking up.

"I HATE YOU!" spluttered Stevie, going pink. He switched off his tablet and dumped it on the sofa. He always, always, always makes a fuss when it is time to stop playing. Bird says he is addicted to the game.

The biggest fight we've ever had was when Stevie had just started playing and he blew up my entire home-complex, just for fun. I confess, I did cry and I hit him. We were both screaming and yelling. And I got the blame! Even after I'd nearly been Made Extinct. Because in this game, after you've lost your life, you're out for good. MAZZO is so popular they are making BILLIONS of pounds, they just don't need you any more. You have to come back as a wraith or a bit of rock and just sit there. (Though you can buy your way out of it with a new loader code, which costs one hundred pounds.)

Then we had to do our reading and our spellings

and only then, when all these things were done, could we get back out to the Mob. It was pretty dark outside, but the machine, or should I say, Russell, was lit up and humming, its screen glowing a seaweed-green.

"HELLO!" Russell said. "SHALL WE MAKE SOMETHING?" He had sensed us coming in through the door and recognized us. He must have an in-built camera.

"Yes," I said. "Let's go."

"EXCELLENT. PLUG IN THE SCANNER AND INPUT YOUR DATA!"

I don't want to bore you with all the instructions Russell gave us but let me just say that eventually we put Stevie's T-shirt on the scan pad and then this laser-thing moved over it and immediately a picture of the Space Hound came on to the screen.

Russell pinged.

"YOU ARE NOT VERY ADVENTUROUS, ARE YOU? YOU CAN MAKE ANYTHING AND YOU CHOOSE TO START WITH THIS POXY OBJECT?"

"Space Hounds ARE NOT POXY," snapped Stevie in outrage.

"WHAT DO YOU WANT THIS TO BE MADE OF?" asked Russell.

He gave us loads of options. (These were in the instruction booklet as well.) I will tell you what they were, though lists are boring. It won't take long to read.

ceramic dust
metal alloy
titanium alloy
thermoplastic
plaster
paper
photopolymer
plastic powder
silver
steel
polycarbonate
wheat flour
wool fibre

Actually that did take quite a long time.

"What the heck are those?" asked Stevie. "And where in the heck are we going to get them?"

"LOOK IN THE DELIVERY CONTAINER," said Russell.

Stacked in the crate were about forty plastic containers. Each with a label containing an ingredient.

We decided we would make the Space Hound from plastic. Following Russell's instructions, we opened a hopper, weighed the right amount of plastic stuff (which looked like little pink chips) – there were scales included in the crate – and shut the lid.

"EXCELLENT. YOU ARE DOING VERY WELL."

I still found it hard to believe that this machine had a voice. I imagined a man standing in a recording studio, recording every single possible sentence. It must have taken months. And how did they KNOW what to record into the machine in advance?

"How does it work?" asked Stevie.

"THE SCANNER ZAPS OUT A LASER, WHICH MEASURES ALL THE PROPERTIES AND DIMENSIONS," said Russell. "I PROCESS IT AND MAKE YOUR OBJECT."

Russell sounded fed up. Was this possible?

"Is this too complicated for you?" I asked politely.

"I AM *THE* MOST MODERN, SUPER-DUPER MACHINE. I AM CAPABLE OF PRINTING ALMOST ANYTHING, BUT YOU WANT THIS RUBBISH!!"

Stevie looked at me. "Are machines supposed to get grumpy?"

"I'M MORE THAN A MACHINE," said Russell.

"Oh, just get on with it," I said. There was something about talking to a machine that made me ruder than usual.

The mechanical arm came down and, with a low buzz, it started layering pink goo on to the pad beneath.

"How long will it take?" asked Stevie.

"About five hours," I guessed.

"DONE!" said Russell.

There, on the pad, lay a little Space Hound exactly the same size as my hand. It was perfect, from its curly tail, to its integral oxygen tanks and beady black eyes.

"This is just the beginning," breathed Stevie, sounding like a mad character in a film. "What shall we make next?

```
chapters[5].title =
```
"MI5.5";

"But where the heck is Russell, Henderson?"

One hundred and twenty miles away, in a secret, central London office, two people stood on either side of a large oak table. Officer Snow was a short, muscular woman with wild, angry hair and an intense, staring sort of look. She was wearing an extremely smart suit and black, shiny shoes with heels that were as long and deadly as dinosaur teeth.

"It could be anywhere," replied Henderson, a lean, dark man with eyebrows that looked like something that should be kept behind thick glass in a zoo. On his collar was a speck of his morning's porridge, spat out when he had heard the bad news.

Officer Snow quivered with tension.

"The whole point of using this company was to keep this BELOW THE RADAR. I wanted Russell to be moved using impregnable military vehicles, but the *committee*" – she spat out the word – "INSISTED it would attract the wrong sort of attention."

Henderson knew his boss hated committees even more than she hated foreign spies, double agents and weak tea. She was the sort of person who liked to have complete control over everything with absolutely no chatting.

"No one believed it would just GET LOST." Snow stalked over to the window, her calf muscles bulging like tennis balls and her heels leaving little injuries in the worn green carpet.

Henderson nervously rubbed his nose. "It won't stay lost. It's too large. I'm sure the parcel company will find it soon."

MI5.5 Officer Snow made a noise that made Henderson think of a large bear in a dark mood.

"This is a matter of national security, you understand?"

"Of course, ma'am."

The office was in an old, not-charming-but-worn-out, sort of building. The carpet had a chocolate stain that had been ground into it by an army general in the Second World War. Paint was peeling off the walls and the ancient, fat radiators had not worked for thirty years. The walls were covered with framed, faded maps. The only furniture in the room was the huge table (key-gouged and ink-scratched) and about twenty chairs. A fly buzzed lazily against the vast screen that covered most of the back wall.

The screen was showing a picture of an extremely large 3D printer.

RUSSELL 1,000,000.

MI5.5, an offshoot of government intelligence agency, MI5, had been set up five years ago and its job was to keep an eye on the latest technology. Mostly they diddled around on the internet (not easy when you barely had any wifi signal in your office), but they also covered all the rapid developments in science and engineering in the name of Keeping the Nation Safe.

Snow had been surprised when she'd been awarded the top job. She had enough trouble working her toaster, let alone decoding the science blogs and nerd-chat required of a cyber-sleuth, but everyone knew she was a dedicated and ruthless operative. What she wanted, she got, be it the Prime Minister's personal emails, a wire-tap into Buckingham Palace or the secret offshore camera surveillance of every holiday-maker in South Wales.

Snow always got the job done. And she'd been confident that soon she was going to be promoted out of this grotty office and into the sleek European Headquarters of International Secret Service, complete with her own villa and swimming pool in the sun.

But this latest mess put that in jeopardy.

"This is a disaster!" Officer Snow dug her fingernails into the window sill. Her face had turned a deep pink with all the blood rushing about just beneath the surface. "Imagine the threat if it falls into the wrong hands. We could have any old country just knocking out a dozen super-missiles or deadly brain interceptors or armed vegetables."

"Armed vegetables, ma'am?"

"Oh, keep up! Tiny nano-cameras infused within the cell work of broccoli, that sort of thing."

"I see," said Henderson, feeling rather blind. Science was not his thing. He liked the old days when all he'd had to worry about were guns, bombs, spies and expenses.

"The bad guys love armed vegetables," said Officer Snow. "We're already a joke. Everyone thinks MI5.5 is *très hilaire*, now we've pooed this up, the whole unit is in jeopardy."

Snow gazed out of the window at the Thames rushing muddily by and ducked in irritation as the fly swooped noisily past.

"Tell me everything you know."

Henderson cleared his throat and began. "At 1400 hours, RUSSELL 1,000,000 was collected from Ministry of Defence HQ by armed soldiers and delivered to the address marked 'B'.

"From here, a private courier was to deliver the

package to Address C. The company collected it at 1500 hours and then the trail goes blank. The machine never arrived and the couriers concerned say the two delivery drivers have gone on holiday. Then Address C receive a parcel, open it, and find it is…"

"What did you say it was, Henderson?"

"Some sort of cage for a large rodent, ma'am. Probably rabbits."

Officer Snow made a funny, grimacing sort of face and swiped at the pestering fly. Still thinking on ursine lines, Henderson imagined a grizzly bear with chewing gum stuck to its hairy chin.

Snow picked up a wad of paper from the table and waved it in Henderson's face.

"Wake up, Dolly Daydream. A rabbit hutch! Do you know how much this printer cost?"

Henderson shook his head.

"It has taken five years of research and five billion pounds to develop. FIVE BILLION POUNDS. It is one of a kind. An international prototype. The Americans are going to be furious. So are the Russians," she added. "Everyone has had a stake in this."

"Things often get lost in the post," said Henderson.

"The machine weighs half a tonne!" Snow roared. "How can you possibly 'lose' that?"

Wadding her papers, she span round and splatted the fly messily against the radiator.

"Do everything in your power to track it down," she ordered. "Use all military equipment required. I suspect it has fallen into the hands of ruthless and deadly agents who intend to use the machine for truly evil deeds."

"So you think it was planned?" asked Henderson nervously. "It didn't just get lost?"

"Of course it was planned. It has to be an international criminal conspiracy." She sat on a creaky, ancient chair, clicked open her laptop and began typing.

"These people are very well organized, very well formed and extremely dangerous."

"OK, ma'am."

Officer Snow closed her eyes.

Russell had national secrets embedded within its code. Things she hadn't admitted to Agent Henderson.

For example, Russell had internet links to every road traffic light in the country, which had all been fitted with secret cameras to keep an eye on things. This also meant that Russell, if it wanted, could turn every light RED in the country at once. If the printer had fallen into enemy hands, the whole country could literally be brought to a standstill. It could be even worse if Russell made them all green. Everyone would crash into each other. Amber would be even worse as everyone in the country would be dithering at once. A mass dither. The country would be a laughing stock.

But that was NOTHING compared to the data the machine held on the secret underground tunnels of the English Channel, let alone the ability to print bombs (Officer Snow swallowed) or space craft.

It really was a devastatingly powerful machine.

"I am authorizing maximum force to get it back," growled Snow. "We must do anything. ANYTHING."

Henderson blinked. "Not *really* anything, ma'am?"

Snow shot to her feet and gazed menacingly at him. Although she only reached his chest, he felt her eyes boring into him and was conscious she could see right into his nostrils. He took a step back and tripped over his lunchbox.

Snow chuffed like a runaway train.

"Oh, do step up, Henderson. The security of our nation is at stake. I want these punks hauled in, TOP PRIORITY."

```
chapters[6].title =
```
"Bird and the Drone";

"Catch!" Stevie chucked the Space Hound to me, so I lobbed it back. Then we had a brutal wrestling session on the bare floor of the Mob.

"Over here, on the head!" shouted Stevie, wriggling free.

I drew back my foot and dropped the Space Hound and booted hard. Stevie leaped up to head it, missed, and the Space Hound went cracking into the Mob window.

"Boys!"

We froze.

It was Mum. Come from nowhere like a deadly fog.

I was first to rouse myself. I ran out of the Mob, dragging my brother and closing the door behind us.

Mum stood, baby Ella in her arms.

"It's bedtime. What's happening in there?"

"School project," we said together.

Mum shrieked as there was a sudden whirring sound. A metal machine hovered above us, blinking yellow and red lights. Its blades whizzing round and round like a tiny, demented helicopter.

Mum snorted. "I hate, HATE those things."

It was a drone and for the last couple of weeks, it had kept coming back. It felt like we were being spied on. It was like being in a James Bond film.

"If that thing fell out of the sky it would kill someone," said Mum, putting a protective hand over Ella's head. The drone hovered a little longer, then went high, high up into the dark sky until it looked like another star.

"When I'm Prime Minister I am going to ban those things," Mum snarled.

"SSSS, Gas-min," said Ella.

"You're like the human equivalent of DOS, that prehistoric operating-system." Bird, our sister, appeared on the kitchen step. "If you were Prime Minister, you'd have us going around in a horse-and-cart instead of cars. We'd eat our lunch by candlelight and play cards in the evenings instead of TV and computers."

"That all sounds quite nice," said Mum.

"Cavewoman," said Bird. "It's time to come out of the Dark Ages."

"Not if I'm going to get spied on by flying machines," grumbled Mum, peering into the sky. "So, can I see this school project?"

Neither Stevie nor I answered.

"Oh." Mum looked thoughtful. "I think that means you don't want me to see."

Stevie nodded.

"Very mysterious." Mum smiled. "Oh, well, as long as it's nothing mad or bad, I don't need to know your secrets."

"Thanks," I said, feeling shifty.

"I'll see you indoors in five minutes," said Mum.

We watched her stride back to the house, Piggy bounding beside her and Ella waving over her shoulder.

But Bird wasn't going anywhere.

"What on earth are you up to?" she demanded, clutching her phone.

"Nothing," said Stevie and I in unison.

"Not nothing. There's been a massive hike in our energy usage. My meter has gone ballistic."

A few years ago, Bird had wired up an energy tracker to the fuse board so we could see how much mains electricity we were using. She had a mission for the household to produce as much of our own electricity as possible, and in the last couple of years had asked for solar panels for her birthday and Christmas and rigged up the small windmill generator at the end of the garden, which made enough electricity to light the whole house.

"My tracker says the energy is being used in the Mob," frowned Bird. "It's like you're boiling twenty kettles in there."

The thing you need to know about my sister is that she's like a bloodhound. She will seek out the answers to her questions and stop at nothing until she gets results.

Me and Stevie did not stand a chance.

"We're just messing about," said Stevie, who evidently believed we still might be able to hide our secret. But this was Bird, not Mum. Our sister did not respect secrets.

Bird retied her bun. She had this brown, spongy thing, which from a distance looked a bit like a fat hamster doughnut. She pulled her hair through the hole and wrapped it round and, using girl-sorcery, fastened it with nails and string, I mean, grips and bands.

"You tripped the trip switch," she said, forcing the bun into submission. "We had a power cut. I told Mum it was my new build."

Bird's latest project involved scavenging lots of old circuits and motherboards from the city dump. Her big idea was to turn the whole house into a kind of super-computer. So now, padded electrodes under our the soles of our slippers generated electricity, as did the mini water-wheels under all the taps.

"SO?" said Bird, flicking her sideways fringe out of her eyes.

Me and Stevie gave each other the Long Look. I was

staring into Stevie's little red face, right into his sparky eyes. This Long Look means we were reading each other's minds.

She will find out anyway, thought Stevie.

She will be excited about it, thought I. *She might help us make something really cool.*

Yeah, but what if she tells Mum and calls the police before we can do anything? thought Stevie.

She wouldn't do that, but she will take over, I thought.

We won't let her, thought Stevie. *We are two and she is but one.*

We will never surrender, thought I. *We will be united against her might.*

Then we stopped the Look.

Bird had folded her arms and was tapping her foot. "Have you finished your little mind-chat?" she asked. For she knew most things about us. Even the fact we were having silent conversations.

"Show me your secret."

"Don't worry," I whispered to Stevie. "I won't let her take over."

chapters[7].title =
"Bird Takes Over";

"Wow, what a beast!" Bird stood before Russell and her eyes grew round and shiny. "What is it? NO, don't tell me. Let me guess." She walked slowly round the machine. She eyed the scan pad. Then she went on to her tiptoes to examine the hoppers. A slow smile spread over her face.

"Oh, ho, ho," she said. I think she'd forgotten we were even here. "Hellooo, baby."

Me and Stevie swapped pained looks. We didn't think Russell would like being called "baby". I was expecting him to say something. He was switched on after all.

"PROPERTY OF THE MOD," read Bird. She shot me a look. "DO NOT TAMPER."

She ran her finger over the production plate and examined the pink dust left there from the Space Hound.

Then she stood back and folded her arms.

"You've got a 3D printer. But I've never heard of anything as elaborate as this. Where did you get it? Does it function? Does Mum know?"

I quickly explained that it had been delivered by mistake and that, no, Mum most definitely did NOT know about it.

"The owners will be looking for it," said Bird. "Something like this must cost hundreds and thousands and billions of pounds. We're probably being hunted by the army. Any minute a Special-Ops team will drop down on ropes from military helicopters and we'll be airlifted away and slammed into army prisons." Bird grinned. "So shall we try and build something first?"

"We already have," I said, desperate to claw back control. Stevie drew out his Space Hound.

"Hmm," said Bird, taking it from him. "You can

print anything in the world and you make a toy? Where's your vision? Why didn't you use the simple animatronics function?"

"We're planning to make something very BIG next," I lied bravely. "Something amazing."

"Like what?" Bird grinned. "A violin? A prefabricated house? A kidney?"

"A kidney?" Stevie made a puking noise into his hand. "Gross, gross, gross. I was planning on making some new Lego."

"Oh, that's stale," said Bird. "This is an extremely special machine. I think we can try something a bit more interesting than Lego."

"Like what?" I asked.

"Well, how about a new leg for Aunty Vi?"

(Our cat was called Aunty Vi and only had three legs.)

"Or let's try and replicate a human hand. Or maybe we could download the algorithm to make a jet pack so we could fly over the houses. Or..."

She bit her bottom lip. "I'm going to have to think about this." She hurried to the door.

"OUCH!"

She sucked her wrist where Dad's nail had caught her.

"Someone pull that thing out." She slammed the door.

There was a very noisy silence. Russell was humming, Stevie was breathing heavily and Piggy was sitting outside the door, nibbling and licking his paws.

"WHO WAS THAT?" Russell blurted out.

"My sister, Bird," said Stevie.

I took his elbow. "Mate, I don't think we should tell it things. I mean, we don't know who it is."

"He's a machine!" replied Stevie. "And he's a he, not an IT."

"Yeah, but don't give out any personal information." I paused. "It's like personal safety on the internet, innit?"

"But we're not on the internet," protested Stevie. "We're in the Mob. Anyway, we know what we're going to print next."

"We do?" I asked.

"Sweets, of course," said Stevie. "What else matters?"

But then Mum came marauding back and so we had to fly out of the Mob before she SAW and we had to go to boring bed and boring sleep and then school and all that stuff which gets in the way of real life.

```
chapters[8].title =
```

"The Second Print Job";

So it was the next evening before we could continue with our printing adventure.

I'd had football practice and Stevie was already chatting to Russell when I arrived, panting and muddy-kneed, in the Mob.

Stevie grinned greedily when he saw me.

"Are you ready for a MOUNTAIN of sweets, bro? We're gonna print chews and sherbet and lollipops and chocolate and jelly beans and barley sugars and humbugs and mints and gum and everything!"

"Oh, yes!" I said. My mouth was already watering. We were only allowed sweets on Fridays. It drove me mad to see other kids slurping up their jellied snakes after school or popping Mini Eggs when the teachers weren't looking. Some kids had sweets EVERY day. Mum says sweets rot our teeth and make us crazy, but they are so delicious that who cares? I gave Russell a warm look.

"WHAT DO YOU WANT FIRST?" asked Russell. The screen was scrolling through pictures of various sweets: boxes of Cadbury's creme eggs, tubes of Smarties, packs of chocolate buttons, jars of green sours. "I HAVE SUGAR SOLUTION AND COLOURANTS."

"I've been thinking about it all day," said Stevie. He held his tablet to Russell's camera. On the screen now was a list of ingredients of those tasty, chewy, yellow, rectangular sweets called Freshies.

Russell clicked and blinked and began printing. In less than ten seconds a perfect yellow sweet sat on the production plate.

"TRY IT," said Russell.

"I'll try it," I said, pushing Stevie's grasping little hand away. "It might be dodgy. I don't want you puking everywhere."

"IT IS PERFECTLY EDIBLE," said Russell, sounding huffy. I took the sweet from the production plate and cautiously licked a corner. It tasted sweet and delicious so I crammed the whole thing into my mouth, dribbled and stuck my thumbs up.

"Hurrah!" said Stevie. "Print more. LOADS more!"

As we watched, Russell printed more sweets, lining them up in rows. He did a batch of fifty in thirty seconds, the needle whirring back and forth in a blur.

"We're going to need papers or they'll get sticky," I said, my mouth still full of yellow goo.

"Omm, uff uff." Stevie had put three sweets in his mouth at once.

"I CAN PRINT WRAPPERS," said Russell. "WHAT DO YOU WANT THEM TO LOOK LIKE?"

So half an hour later we had about five thousand sweets and were steadily wrapping them in paper. I'd done about thirty and Stevie had done five. We didn't care about the colour of the wrappers so they were just plain blue.

"This is quite boring," spluttered Stevie, his mouth full. His hair had yellow lumps glued into it. His favourite elephant T-shirt was blotchy with sugar and yellow slime. My fingers were sticky with dust and paper but the sweets were piled on Stevie's red plastic sledge and they smelled amazing and tasted delicious, as good as the real thing.

We decided we'd had enough of them for now and got Russell to print us lollipops, the boiled-sugar, see-through, orange kind, that crack like coloured glass when you bite them. Russell was doing this clever thing where first he printed the sticks, then the lolly straight on to them. He'd already done a thousand.

I felt like a king, though my mouth was beginning to go numb and I also felt a little bit sick, but I could not stop eating. Stevie said he had a sore spot on his gum, but he could not stop eating either. The orange lollies were lovely, though once I was on my fourth, my tongue was burning and I had to have a break.

I was starting to think we had printed too many. How would we ever eat them all?

"We can SELL them," said Stevie, reading my

mind. His plan was to charge fifty pence for twenty sweets.

"We're going to be millionaires!" shouted Stevie, dancing round the Mob and making the windows rattle.

"What will you buy?" I asked.

"More sweets!" replied Stevie.

Bird hadn't yet returned to the Mob. She had science club on a Tuesday and usually hung around afterwards with her dopey friends. I wondered what *she* would come up with. It was bound to be something wacky and zany. Would it be a self-playing musical instrument? A pair of flying shoes? A ground-breaking energy-saving device? A wind-up space rocket?

We were having a restful game of football, much more difficult now Russell took up a chunk of my indoor pitch, when Bird finally returned to the Mob, carrying her laptop.

"WOW." She took in the piles of lollies and chews. "Can I try one?"

Whatever she was planning to make, she didn't

say. Bird was also fond of sweets and had a courageous attempt at denting the mountain. She laughed when we said we were going to sell them and said we would get caught, but she didn't try to stop us. She was quite helpful and managed to wrap eighty sweets before bedtime.

I realized that Russell was being very quiet. Sure, I'd only known him for a short while but I had worked out he was a very opinionated machine. He liked talking. But he hadn't said a word for ages.

"Russell, why are you so quiet?"

"Maybe he's scared of girls," suggested Stevie, who sometimes suffered from this himself.

"He talks?" Bird stopped wrapping and looked excited. "What does he say? Does he have a monotone voice? An old person's voice? What is his accent?"

"It's just a bloke-voice," I replied. "An English accent, sort of slightly northern."

"He told us he was more than a machine," remembered Stevie. "He said that printing toys was beneath him."

"Wow." Bird gave Russell a searching look. "The

printer is sentient!" She frowned. "You're keeping your cards close to your chest, aren't you?"

It was not a question. She sounded like she was accusing it.

"What's sentient?" asked Stevie.

"Being sensible," I replied. "I think."

"Not me then," said Stevie brightly.

Bird leaned very close to Russell.

"Here's a camera, so it can see exactly who we are and what we are doing." She pulled at the lens and it popped out a little. "Hmm, it's on a retractable stem. So it can see all round the Mob and probably out of the window too. Here is the microphone, so it can hear us talking. A machine of this quality probably has a translation tool. I wouldn't be surprised if it can speak and understand most of the major language groups. I suspect it has GPS tracking, which means who ever created this or owns it should know exactly where it is."

"Oh, no!" I said, alarmed. "Then the owners could be here any minute?"

"Of course," said Bird. "If we want some fun, we'd really better get cracking. Machines of this calibre don't just turn up in people's Mobs." She peered again into the lens. "You're being very, very quiet, oh, machine. Can you really talk?"

"Maybe he's scared of you because you know so much about him," suggested Stevie. "Me and Olly are too thick for him to worry about."

"HELLO, BIRD." Russell suddenly broke his silence. "APOLOGIES. MY TALK FUNCTION SOMETIMES HAS A BLIP."

"I don't believe you," said Bird.

"THAT IS UNFORTUNATE," said Russell, sounding huffy.

"Has she just accused a *printer* of lying?" I whispered to Stevie.

"Yup," said Stevie.

"I knew we shouldn't let her get involved," I said.

Then Mum was yelling about dinner and all action had to stop.

We had to sneak past her to wash the sticky sweet stuff off and when she learned that Stevie was having a shower without being forced, her face clouded with suspicion.

My teeth hurt, my tongue felt hot and sore and I knew if I ate one more sweet I would be very ill.

It had been the best day EVER.

Meanwhile, one hundred and twenty miles away...

"Got it!" MI5.5 Officer Snow thumped the table. "We'll check the GPS satellite positioning."

Henderson looked pained. Yet again, he was going to have to disappoint his boss.

"No can do, ma'am. It was disabled before the journey to stop enemies tracking and hijacking the machine."

"Oh, for goodness' sake!" Snow rubbed her forehead. "Why haven't you tracked down the delivery drivers yet?"

"Their relatives said they'd both gone on their holidays. No one knows exactly where."

Snow's face darkened. "It sounds like a scam. You will go to their homes and conduct a thorough search. There must be some paperwork telling us the flight information. Then we'll send a Special Ops team to

Spain or Brazil, or wherever, and we'll drag them back here and get the truth out of them!"

"I don't know if we can send a team to Brazil, ma'am," said Henderson nervously. "It breaks international protocol." He waited for the eruption.

"I DON'T CARE. JUST DO IT!" howled Snow. "I'll DO WHATEVER IT TAKES TO GET THAT MACHINE BACK. EVEN I HAVE TO BREAK A DOZEN INTERNATIONAL LAWS!"

Her phone pinged and she checked the screen. She grunted a slightly pleased grunt.

"Good news, ma'am?" asked Henderson shyly.

Snow grunted again. "My son has just achieved level eight on MAZZO. It means he can own Space Hounds."

"That's amazing, ma'am. I myself cannot progress beyond level four."

Snow did not admit that she had not progressed beyond level four either, despite playing on the way home on the Tube every day. She shook herself.

"FIND THAT MACHINE!"

chapters[9].title =
"The Third Print Job";

The next morning, Mum left early to take Ella to nursery before she went to work. Mum has her own business making and selling ladies pants. Big ones.

"Nice knickers for the older woman!" Mum explains to everyone. "Pretty pants so you can wade through a stream with style and hold in your dinner at the same time."

You can imagine the hell I get at school.

Loads of people want to buy her pants so she gets them made in a factory in Poland and they get sent over here to her "unit", which is like a mini-mini-mini warehouse on the edge of town. Mum also has a big van. It's extremely embarrassing because it is usually parked outside our house and has brightly printed sides.

* BLOOMERS * WELL MADE * SECURE * GORGEOUS *

Then there's a big, colourful picture of flowery knickers. It's so humiliating.

Bird had also left before I'd even come downstairs. She'd gone to her weekly Dawn Coders Club. So when I arrived in the kitchen there was just Stevie, steadily working his way through a box of cereal, without bothering with a bowl, spoon or milk.

It was still only 7.30 a.m. We had an hour before we had to leave for school.

"Shall we make something?" asked Stevie. His hair was flattened on one side where he'd been sleeping.

I ran my tongue over my teeth, which still felt furry from all that sugar yesterday.

"Let's do it," I said, grabbing a couple of slices of bread from the bag and cramming them into my mouth.

The Mob was chilly in the mornings and the windows were steamed up with condensation. It always smelled a bit too, of old carpets and old dinners. Now it smelled very strongly of burned sugar. I eyed the mountain of blue-wrapped sweets on the table. I wouldn't eat one even if someone paid me five pounds.

Probably.

The red light over Russell's scan pad winked on and off very fast as we approached.

"GOOD MORNING! WHAT SHALL I MAKE FOR YOU?" asked Russell.

"It's your turn," said Stevie, still clutching his box of cereal.

"OK," I said.

The thing was, I didn't know. It had kept me awake last night, wondering about it. What did I want? I had a skateboard and a bicycle. I didn't want to make something huge, like a house, because Mum would find out. I would have liked a jet pack, so I could fly, but something told me that wasn't a good idea. Of course I'd like a gun, but that was a very bad idea with Stevie around. My hobbies were football, swimming and reading comics. How could Russell help me with those?

I had toyed with the idea of printing a drum kit, a mini replica tank and a giant inflatable castle. All would be fun. But where to begin? It was like being given a mountain of presents and not knowing where to start.

But what I really, really wanted was ... a swimming pool.

"You WHAT?" spluttered Stevie. "How? YES. But how?"

I had thought about it. Obviously, if we put a swimming pool in the garden, Mum would notice. But I had a plan.

"You want to put a swimming pool in *here*?" squeaked Stevie.

I nodded.

"Why not?"

The Mob was about six metres across and twenty metres long, about as long as a double decker bus and twice as wide. The main room used to be a sitting room and a kitchen and a bedroom before Dad took the walls down. I reckoned I could get a nice little pool in here, leaving plenty of room for Russell.

"You're so crazy," grinned Stevie, breakfast cereal bits stuck to his teeth. "Let's start right away."

Russell blinked and whirred and said that it would be very easy to make us a swimming pool to fit, but that he did not want to get wet and, also, did we think the floor would hold several tonnes of water?

I explained how the Mob was sitting on a concrete base, so I was sure it would be fine.

"How will we fill it?" asked Stevie. "Russell can't print water."

"With the hose, dopey," I said. I assured Russell that we would not let him get wet.

"We'll put a bin liner or something over you," said Stevie comfortingly.

"I DO NOT WANT A BIN LINER OVER ME," huffed Russell.

"Oh, it will be OK," I said. "We'll just make sure we do dive bombs at the other end."

I felt my mouth stretching into a huge grin. This was going to be amazing.

"WHAT ARE 'DIVE BOMBS?" asked Russell. "I DO NOT PRINT EXPLOSIVES FOR CHILDREN."

And so we had to explain that too.

"How will you do it?" asked Stevie.

"I WILL TAKE MEASUREMENTS OF THIS STRUCTURE AND CONSTRUCT WATERPROOF PANELS ACCORDINGLY. THESE WILL SLOT TOGETHER TO CREATE A LEAKPROOF MEMBRANE." Russell paused. "YOU WILL NEED TO PUT IT TOGETHER."

"No problem," I said. I liked making things. "It'll be like giant Lego."

"I'll START RIGHT AWAY," said Russell.

But then the alarm beeped on my phone, which meant, VERY sadly, we had to go to school.

"NO!" shrieked Stevie. "We absolutely CAN'T go to school. The excitement is KILLING ME. How will I bear to sit in that place all day for hours and HOURS when we could be doing THIS?"

"I know," I said. I felt the same way.

"We could skip school?" said Stevie, putting his head to one side, batting his eyelashes and trying to look sweet.

I thought about this. Mum trusted us. If we did not

go to school she would probably find out and then we would have to endure a living death of no MAZZO, no TV, no SKYPE and no biscuits for at least a week. So, with great reluctance, I hauled Stevie out of the Mob and got us both to school before the bell went.

chapters[10].title=

"The Wise Young Boy of the Mid-lands";

We ran home, as fast as if a pack of howling teachers were behind us. We dumped our bags just inside the gate and flew round the back and crashed into the Mob door like a couple of sweaty wrecking balls.

Stevie and me had to throw all our weight against the door to open it a crack and squeeze ourselves through. The first thing I noticed was the stench of hot plastic, the second, that the centre of my Mob was filled, nearly to the ceiling, with a vast roll of blue, bendy stuff.

"HELLO, BOYS," said Russell. "YOUR POOL IS READY TO ASSEMBLE."

"It doesn't look much like a swimming pool," said Stevie, his little red face drooping with disappointment.

"Nothing looks like what it is until it is what it is," I said, which I thought sounded incredibly wise.

Maybe I was incredibly wise and I hadn't known it until now. I could be the Wise Young Boy of the Mid-Lands. People would come to me to buy spells and hear my wisdom.

"Ol-leee, where's the blimmin' pool?" huffed Stevie.

A Wise Young Boy would know how to piece together a freshly printed swimming pool. And so I examined the nearest blue section. It was flat and thin and about half a metre wide. On one side the edge was grooved, on the other there was a little lip.

"SLOT IT TOGETHER," said Russell. "I PRINTED IT IN ONE CONTINUOUS PIECE. THE EDGES ARE COMPOSED OF A FABRIC WHICH, ON CONTACT, WILL MESH AT AN ATOMIC LEVEL."

"I see," I lied.

"I don't," said Stevie. "What is 'meshing at an atomic level'?"

Bird would know. I wished she was here.

"IT MEANS YOUR POOL WILL NOT LEAK," explained Russell.

I found the end of the roll wedged against the sink and I tugged it out, making the whole room vibrate with a wobble-noise. It was a bit like unrolling a carpet. Stevie helped me shove the roll around the room, unspooling as we went. When we got back to the beginning, we heaved up the roll and fitted it on top of the first layer. It was like putting a giant apple peeling back on the apple. I don't know about the atomic stuff but the layers meshed beautifully as we laid it down.

After our third trip around the room, the sides were finished. Russell was busy printing the bottom of the pool.

Within half an hour we had a neat little swimming pool, which took up two-thirds of my Mob. Though of course we couldn't swim in it as it had no water. So, technically, it wasn't a swimming pool yet. It could become a wetlands turtle farm or a waterproof science space or…

"Wow," said Stevie. "Thanks! It is a brilliant swimming pool."

"YOU ARE THE FIRST PEOPLE TO THANK ME FOR ANYTHING," replied Russell. "PEOPLE NEVER THANK MACHINES."

"These people will from now on," breathed Stevie, his eyes shining.

Then it was just a matter of filling it up. I nipped outside and dragged the hosepipe from its reel on the garden wall. It wouldn't stretch through the Mob door so instead I wedged it in the window, the end waggling over the pool. Piggy was barking like mad all the time I was doing this. I think he could sense the great excitement in the air.

"Do it, do it, do it," chanted Stevie, already in his goldfish swimming trunks and neon-green goggles.

I ran back through the garden and turned on the tap at the wall.

A few seconds later there was a whoop of ecstasy from the Mob.

Inside I found Stevie, jittering and gasping under a cascade of water as it shot out from the hose above him. I squeezed through the door and watched as my brother lay down and did a lively backstroke in a puddle.

"AWESOME," he yelled. I pulled off my shirt and trousers and jumped in to join him, wearing just my pants. The water was freezing. (Too late, I realized I had forgotten to take my socks off.) The puddles grew bigger and bigger but after five minutes the bottom of the pool was still not covered. It was going to take ages to fill. We didn't mind. There was enough water to kick into each other's faces. We got this game going where you had to try and flatten the other person so they lay in the cold water.

Obviously I won.

We were doing running skids through the waterfall and screaming like mad ferrets when the door opened and Bird looked in.

"Hmm," she said.

"JOIN US," howled Stevie, scooping up a handful of water and flinging it at her.

Bird moved her head to one side and the water dribbled down the wall.

"Not on your life," she said. She paused. "This will use an obscene amount of water. And it will start going smelly in a few days as there appears to be no filtration."

"Ya, ya, ya." I skidded over to her. "Come and swim like a crazy moonlit monk."

"I will consider it when it is full," said Bird. She fingered the side of the pool. Then, unexpectedly, she smiled.

"This is very cool. Well done. Don't drown."

The door tapped shut and Bird had gone.

We quickly forgot about her because the floor of the pool was now so slippery it was very easy to drag one's brother around by a leg.

"WHAT IS IT CALLED? WHAT YOU ARE DOING NOW?" piped up Russell from underneath the cobwebby old tent flysheet we'd hauled over him.

"IT IS NOT SWIMMING, SO WHAT IS IT?"

"We're playing, you buffoon," said Stevie, and tripped me over for fun.

Half an hour later and the pool was covered in about two centimetres of water. We leaned, shivering, over the side (we had no towels), watching the water deepen impossibly slowly.

"I'm bored," said Stevie.

"Me too," I said. "Let's go and play MAZZO."

We scampered back to the house, leaving Russell in charge. Mum saw us dart, half-dressed, through the kitchen but she was on the phone and trying to feed Ella mushed-up carrots so she didn't say anything except that it was dinner in ten minutes.

She's used to our mysterious ways.

It was eight o'clock at night before the pool was full. Mum was giving Ella a bath so we were safe.

The water shimmered in the evening light. We drew the curtains, locked the Mob door and slithered in.

The cold took my breath away and I came up screeching and gasping. Then I did a quick lap around the edges. It took about fifteen seconds. After that I didn't feel so cold.

"This has been the best day of my life," said Stevie, floating past on his inflatable turtle. He lifted his head. "Do you think Russell could print me a snorkel?"

At bedtime Mum ran her hand over my head.

"Have you just had a shower without being asked?" she asked, looking confused.

"Sort of," I said, and scampered off before there were any more questions.

That night I could barely sleep, I was so excited. I couldn't believe we had our very own swimming pool. I was thinking about how Raz could come back after school and have a swim. He was pretty good at keeping secrets.

When I woke early the next morning, I thought the whole swimming pool thing must have been a dream. I listened for silence, then crept downstairs in my pyjamas. There was no one in the kitchen except Piggy, who gave me a happy wag of his tail, so I unbolted the back door and stepped, barefoot, into the garden.

It was a bright, sparkling sort of morning and I heard birds singing in the trees and the milkman's van gliding along the street.

I opened the door of the Mob and peered into the water. The surface of the pool danced with light and patterns.

I hadn't dreamed it.

```
chapters[11].title =
```

"A Word with the Head";

When I got to school I just had to tell Raz. We were rummaging in our drawers for our topic books when I whispered that he should come over after school because we had a secret swimming pool in the Mob.

Of course he didn't believe me.

"This is just another of your wild ideas," he said.

"It's NOT," I said loudly, earning myself a glare from our teacher. "Come and see for yourself."

Then we got swept up in volcanoes and earthquakes and the other disasters that Mrs McCurdy liked to inflict on us.

Five minutes before the lunch bell, the headmistress,

Mrs Melle, came into our classroom. She nodded at our teacher and then, to my amazement, called my name.

"Olly Fugue, I'd like a word."

And so I had to follow her out of the class. I sensed everyone looking at me, wondering what was going on. *I* was wondering what was going on. Was everyone OK? Had I won a prize? (Unlikely.) Had I done something wrong? (Not as far as I knew.) Had THEY discovered Russell?

Mrs Melle's office was tucked behind the staffroom and overlooked the playground. From the window I could see the school cooks opening the doors of the canteen ready for lunch. My stomach rumbled in either hunger or unease, or maybe both.

"Sit," ordered Mrs Melle. She wore a grey suit and there were threads of grey in her shiny black bob. Her blue-framed glasses magnified her brown eyes. I hadn't taken much notice of her in my school career, nor she of me, and that was how I liked it. I felt very out of place, like a horse at the dentist's.

I sat, warily, in a hard, plastic chair, facing her

desk. The wall was covered with certificates for this and that. But there was also a postcard of a snowy mountain.

"Snowdonia," said Mrs Melle, watching me.

Someone knocked at the door.

"Come in." Mrs Melle pulled up a second chair next to mine as a very scared-looking Stevie sidled in. He looked so worried that I felt sorry for him. Stevie isn't very big.

When he saw me his face cracked in relief.

This HAD to be about Russell.

Mrs Melle gestured for Stevie to sit, then she opened a drawer and brought out a plastic shopping bag. She tipped it up and emptied a large heap of our blue-wrapped sweets on her desk.

"Recognize these?" she asked.

Was this a trick?

Neither of us said anything. I hadn't taken them to school. We hadn't decided when or where to sell them. The swimming pool had taken up all of our brain space.

"Stevie, you were selling these at break time. It is

against school rules to bring sweets on to the premises. It is against school rules to run a market stall in the playground. Does your mum know about this?"

We shook our heads.

Stevie looked at me apologetically.

Sorry! he thought-spoke. *I sold loads before I was caught.*

IDIOT, I thought back. *Don't say anything about Russell. Let me do the talking.*

"I understand you sold Kitty Evans twenty sweets!" said Mrs Melle. "You will give her back her money."

"Sorry," said Stevie.

"Where did you get them?" asked the headmistress. "I've never seen anything like them."

"I got them," I broke in, so that Stevie didn't give us away. "I ordered them on the internet. It's my fault."

Good man. Thanks, thought-spoke Stevie.

You owe me, I replied silently.

"All right," said Mrs Melle. "I will let this go, if you promise not to bring this sort of rubbish into school again. Also, tonight, instead of football, you will pick litter on the school field, Olly."

Everyone knew that I loved football. "OK," I said.

She held up a sweet.

"You can collect these at the end of the day," she said.

"Oh, you can keep them," I said, thinking of the mountain of sweets in my Mob.

"No, thank you," said Mrs Melle firmly.

So I ended up with a detention after school and Stevie got away with just a telling-off. I expect he'll manage to pay me back by the end of the next century. I had to watch as all my mates charged around tackling and scoring, while I picked up empty crisp bags and apple cores. And Stewart Grimsby did thirty keepie-uppies and got a badge! I can do fifty easily. I was desperate to join in, but of course I couldn't.

When I finally got home the house was empty. On Thursday nights Ella stays late at nursery as Mum usually works at her unit. Bird brings Stevie home. I dropped my bag on the doormat and went straight to the cupboard and made myself a jam sandwich and a cup of tea.

I was munching my sandwich when I heard something. It was a shout and it was coming from the garden.

When I opened the back door, I saw the door of the Mob was hanging open. I could actually see the blue side of the pool.

The noise was even louder. I could hear splashing and laughing. I hurried down to my Mob, climbed the steps and looked inside.

I could not believe what I saw.

You would not believe it either.

It was unbelievable.

chapters[12].title =
"The School Outing";

The pool was packed with kids from my school. Raz waved at me from the far end. Henrietta Stibbens burst up from underwater. Davey, Yolanda, Chance, Harris, Jayden, Bonni, Chandrak, Will, Lee, Gunjeet, Sid – nearly my whole class was here! There was barely space for them to move around but they were managing to play some kind of water polo game.

Stevie grinned at me from the side.

"Raz asked me about the pool," he said. "Word got out."

"You were telling the truth!" shouted Raz happily

and batted the ball so hard it slammed into the wall.

"Love the pool, Olly!" called Henrietta Stibbens. The pack of girls she was with were all giggling, doing handstands and booting the ball around and ducking any boy who came near.

I couldn't speak. Surely now Mum would discover everything and this whole thing would be over. I looked at my watch. She would be home in twenty minutes. There would be no hiding this. Even Piggy was doggy-paddling at the far end..

I felt a hand on my shoulder. It was Bird. She was wearing a long, red dress, blue lipstick and green wellies.

She patted my arm.

"Don't panic," she said. "We can sort this out."

I think the next fifteen minutes were the craziest of my whole life.

First, Bird stood on the side and shouted,

"SOMEONE HAS WEED IN THE POOL! I CAN SEE IT!"

Had they?

"No," said Bird, reading my mind.

But it worked. Everyone started making "arrrrgh" noises and clambering out.

"You've all got to go home, fast," shouted Bird. "This pool is a birthday surprise for our mum. She'll be home any minute."

I helped people get out and ran around reuniting them with their shoes and bags and walked them out of the garden and then went back for more and my heart was beating, beating, beating.

A couple of lads, Sid and Raz, were still in the pool when I went to check so I just shouted,

"PLEASE GET OUT!"

Raz took one look at my face and he did.

I got rid of my best friend in three minutes.

Then there was silence. Just Bird, Stevie and me and lots of damp footprints on the garden path. Piggy shook himself and water went everywhere.

Ten seconds later we heard Mum's car pull up on the front driveway. I ran and shut the Mob door.

"Everyone knows now," I said, trembling. "EVERYONE."

"Never panic," said Bird, lifting the hem of her dress out of a puddle.

"Sorry," said Stevie. "Everyone started telling everyone else and then no one could find you."

"Because I was litter picking on the school field," I said.

"And they were all asking me and…"

"Hel-looo?" called Mum. "Where is everyone?"

"Come on," said Bird. "Act natural."

chapters[13].title =

"Russell's Secret";

I was beginning to think we had got away with it. We'd had tea, done our homework, had our MAZZO hour and Mum hadn't even begun to suspect that hordes of my classmates had been recently swimming in the old mobile home at the bottom of her garden.

It was eight-thirty and I was in my pyjamas and watching a little bit of TV when the phone rang.

Mum was in the kitchen doing her paperwork so she answered it.

"Hi, Mo."

"Sorry, I didn't catch that?"

I sat up.

"No."

"WHAT?"

This did not sound good.

"I think someone is pulling your leg."

"NO."

"WHO?"

"WHAT?"

The door of the sitting room flung open. Mum stood there, her eyes wide with shock.

"Olly? What's this about a swimming party?"

I said nothing.

"What's going on?"

In these sorts of moments, I always find silence is the best option. You don't have to get your story straight if you don't tell a story in the first place.

Mum turned on her heel and belted out of the kitchen into the garden. I followed at a distance. I felt curiously calm, though I shut my eyes and felt a twinge in my guts when Mum shouted, "WHY IS IT SO WET?"

The garden was soaked. There were pools of water all over the June-baked grass and a small river was running along the bottom fence where it sloped away.

Mum flung open the Mob door and I waited for my end.

And waited.

And waited.

But my end did not come. Instead, I heard Mum squelching back over to me.

"Why is it so wet?" she repeated. "You'll drown my roses."

I opened one eye. Like that would halve the pain when it came. The pain of the biggest telling-off ever. I saw a slick of water on the Mob steps.

"Have you been playing with the hose?"

I opened the other eye. The ground really was sodden.

Mum had said nothing about the pool.

This was odd. And when I climbed the slippery Mob steps and looked inside, the pool, had … gone…

"You must have gone BERSERK with the hose," snapped Mum, dead-heading a couple of roses. "This place is like a MARSH. Don't waste water and ASK if you want a friend to play." She slipped and slid back to the house and to her spreadsheets.

I stood, utterly confused, watching pools of water lap the lower stems of the giant rhubarb.

It was late before I got to talk to Russell. Mum kept us busy with washing up and homework and then we Skyped Granny. Granny lives on the Isle of Wight, which is a little island off the bottom of England. She owns an antique shop and we only see her about twice a year because she is so busy. We all had a chat, and then Granny started going on about exams and working hard and making life easy for our mother, so Stevie, Bird and I left Mum and Ella to it and snuck out to the Mob. Skyping is good like that – the person on the other end doesn't know you're not actually lurking just out of shot.

The smell hit us as soon as we opened the door. A festering aroma of stale air and wet flooring. I stepped into a puddle and noticed dark stains climbing the damp walls.

No swimming pool.

"WOW," said Stevie. "Where has it gone?"

At the far end, Bird was unwrapping Russell from the tent covering.

"CAN YOU OPEN THE WINDOWS?" he said. "THIS CLIMATE IS VERY BAD FOR ME."

We slipped and skidded over the floor, pushing open all the windows and using discarded towels to mop up the puddles.

"I NEED TO LEAVE THIS PLACE," complained Russell. "IT WILL DESTROY ME."

"Don't touch it," warned Bird. "Water and electricity don't mix. You might get a nasty shock. It could *kill* you."

Me and Stevie gaped at Bird.

"IT'S OK, I AM SITTING ON A RUBBER WATERPROOF MEMBRANE," said Russell. "I STILL DO NOT LIKE THE CLIMATE, BUT I HAVE RESEARCHED THE WEATHER AND IT IS GOING TO BE HOT FOR THE NEXT WEEK, SO THIS PLACE WILL DRY UP."

"But how ... how...?" stammered Stevie.

"Where's the pool?" I asked.

Russell started busily blowing out hot air from his side ventilators. "IT HAS GONE," he announced. "I INCLUDED A 48-HOUR DESTRUCT PATTERN IN THE DESIGN."

"What?"

"How and why did you do that?" asked Bird.

"I DO NOT LIKE WATER. IF THE POOL HAD STAYED FOR MUCH LONGER, I WOULD MALFUNCTION IN THE HUMID CONDITIONS."

"Oh, I see," said Bird. "You are programmed for self-preservation."

"What is she on about now?" asked Stevie. "Where's my pool?"

"This machine will do things without being asked, if it means it will keep itself safe." Bird frowned. "It's rather worrying."

"How did you do it?" I asked. "HOW did you make the pool vanish?"

"I INCLUDED A MELT FUNCTION ALONGSIDE THE MESH FUNCTION," replied Russell. "THE STRUCTURE IS MADE OF A DISSOLVABLE

STARCH. AFTER THE DESIGNATED TIME, IT FOLDED AND DISSOLVED INTO THE H20 CARRYING AGENT."

"It means the structure dissolved into the water," said Bird. "And the water all just ran out of the door into our garden."

"CORRECT," said Russell. "AND I THINK YOU ARE GLAD I DID IT."

"I suppose so," I said. "It was fun, though."

"Can you print another one?" asked Stevie.

Russell said no. He said he wanted no more water anywhere near him. He asked again if we could move him somewhere less damp while the Mob dried up, but of course, we couldn't.

When I went to bed, I stood at my window, looking out at the Mob at the bottom of the garden. It was a big, scruffy old thing, and not especially interesting, apart from the pink and white roses rampantly rambling over it. I shivered a bit, thinking of all the mad things we might make next. There was a soft tap at my door and Bird came in wearing her pyjamas and clutching her laptop, followed by Stevie, who was wrapped in his duvet.

"Where's Mum?" I asked. The baby was in bed already.

"Working downstairs," answered Bird. My sister looked excited and flushed. She nibbled on the corner of her thumb as she quietly shut the door.

"OK," she said. "Very soon, Russell will be discovered."

I nodded. But I still didn't see HOW they would find him. Maybe they would NEVER find him.

"So let's make something AMAZING," breathed Bird. "Something we all really, really want."

"Something we want more than sweets and a swimming pool?" Stevie looked sceptical.

Bird looked at each of us.

"Let's make a DAD."

chapters[14].title =
"The Fourth Print-Job";

There was a pause. My sister's eyes were shining. I thought she had gone mad.

"We'll scan in a photograph. Upload some new dimensions and get a pop-up Dad. He'll look just like the original. It will be a 3D model."

"But why?" asked Stevie.

Bird stopped grinning. "Don't you miss him?"

"Yes but…"

"I miss him too. This way, we'll have a life-sized Dad."

"It's a bit weird," I said. "I'd rather have the real thing."

"Well, so would I," said Bird, annoyed. "But a print-out version is second best." She looked out of the window and this was a sign that she was probably fighting tears.

Out of all of us, I think Bird missed Dad the most. Me and Stevie had got used to him being away with work SO MUCH of the time (before he lost his job). But Bird says he wasn't always like that. She says he used to come home every night and he wouldn't work at weekends. And he used to play. She says sometimes he'd take days off and the two of them would mess around in the park or build stuff together in the Mob, like potato clocks and solar circuits. But when me, and then Stevie, came along, he spent less and less time at home and more and more time at work. And even when he WAS at home, he'd check his phone every few minutes for email messages or nip into the next room to take or make a call.

"Hmm." Stevie was unconvinced. "Will this new Dad be squishy? My Space Hound isn't squishy."

"Not as squishy as the real thing." Bird cleared her throat and turned back to us. Her cheeks blazed with colour. "If we were skilled we could use DNA plasma and artificial skin and build a nearly real Dad. But we're not skilled. So this will have to be made of plastic, I guess."

"He'll be a bit quiet," said Stevie thoughtfully.

"So is the real one," said Bird. Her eyes gleamed. "At least…" I could almost hear her brain whirring. "Wow, imagine if you built a Dad-shell and uploaded all his internet profile and recorded his voice and generated an entire vocabulary and programmed in some general responses. We could put him on a mechanical frame. We could download an animatronics function and make a very basic robot that could walk. You'd get a Dad-borg." Bird chuckled. "He might be even better than the original."

"Program him to say we can play MAZZO on the computer all evening," said Stevie.

"We'll start with the outside," said Bird. "Let's keep it simple to begin with."

I wasn't sure about this. Just thinking about Dad brought up loads of uncomfortable feelings, but Bird had opened her laptop and was typing all the things we needed to do.

<u>Bird's List</u>

1. Scan full-body photo, search setting for 3D version
2. Input Dad's measurements
3. Scale up photo to life-size
4. Find out what extra unprintable parts we need e.g. hair (wig) electrics etc. and order them

The list went on and on and I admit I didn't understand quite a lot of it.

"Electrics?" said Stevie.

"Oh, I'm just covering the bases," said Bird airily.

"What bases?" I asked, suspecting my sister might not be planning to "keep it simple" at all.

"The electric ones," answered Bird.

```
chapters[15].title =
```

"Printing Dad";

So that weekend we printed Dad.

On Saturday morning loads of packages arrived, all addressed to Bird.

"What are all these?" asked Mum.

"Early Christmas shopping," said Bird, smiling, like smiling made it OK to lie to Mum.

"It's June!" said Mum.

"I'm getting organized," said Bird. She'd ordered all this stuff on the internet.

"Raz's mum asked me when we got the swimming pool," said Mum. "I told her there was no pool and she looked really surprised."

"How peculiar," said Bird.

Fortunately, Ella crawled into the washing machine and the phone rang and Aunty Vi the cat was yowling for food, so we took the opportunity to grab all the packages and slip away while Mum was distracted.

The Mob was much dryer now. There were no puddles and the wet had stopped climbing the walls. However, it now smelled like old cats and Russell kept blasting out heat, which Bird said was sending her energy tracker through the roof.

"What *is* in these parcels?" I asked Bird, when we were safely bolted in.

"Bits for Dad." Bird opened one small, white envelope and inside was some blue dye and some extra-strong glue.

"To colour his eyes and to glue on his fingernails," explained Bird.

"Eugh," said Stevie.

Bird had found a really good picture on her laptop. It was taken about five years ago, when Dad still played football at the weekends, and he was wearing his kit, an ancient yellow Wolves shirt and prehistoric boots.

"Can I email this to you?" Bird asked Russell.

"YES," said Russell. "IT'S RUSSELL@RUSSELL.COM."

Bird tapped away and within seconds the image of Dad appeared on Russell's screen.

"Now I'll input the measurements. Do we want to size him up?" asked Bird.

"What?" asked Stevie.

"Do we want to make him bigger?" I explained.

"Do it!" said Stevie. "Dad always wanted to be a bit taller."

Our first plan, to make a big, plastic version of Dad, quickly changed. Russell told us we could make him *soft*, using rubber crystals. Russell also told us we should make him hollow and that we should print a kind of frame or skeleton so that he could stand up. He was also going to have *flexible* limbs.

"Like a giant man-Barbie," said Bird, whose own Barbies had long since been melted down or strung up or turned inside out or simply been raided for "parts" to make something more interesting.

"I CAN TELL YOU EXACTLY WHAT TO DO," said Russell.

"No," said Bird firmly. "We'll tell *you* what to do. You just tell us HOW to make it happen."

And the very first thing we printed was his head.

Russell talked us through every step.

"NOW PUT THE FIBROUS FILAMENT IN HOPPER 3…"

…Stuff like that. I won't go into detail because there was a lot of it. We took it in turns to sit with Russell and feed in the different materials. We used a close-up photograph taken at around the same time as the footballing one. Russell toned the eyes to exactly the right shade of blue. We used a kind of silicone-jelly, which Russell said would make them *gelatinous*.

When Dad's head was finished, I lifted it off the production plate and held it up for the others to see. We pondered it in silence. It was a bit skew-whiff. It looked like Dad's demon brother, with a sick-looking, waxy skin, and the dull, lifeless eyes gave me the shivers. The head was as heavy as a bag of flour and smelled of hot plastic. It was hollow and had a nearly-invisible seam in the back where you could open it, should you wish, which I did.

I was expecting Dad's head to be empty, but inside were five little plug-socket things, one behind each ear and one behind each eye and another at the base of his head.

"What are these, Russ?" I asked.

"IN CASE YOU WANT TO GIVE HIM A BRAIN," replied Russell nonchalantly.

Bird frowned and leaned closer to Russell's camera lens.

"Whose brain?" she asked firmly.

I sat and thought about it. It was all very well printing a man who looked like Dad. But how would we print his brain?

"IT'S ADVANCED," admitted Russell. "BUT IT WOULD BE A BAD DESIGN IF I DIDN'T INCLUDE FUTURE OPTIONAL BRAIN PLUG-INS."

"The thing is, Russell," said Bird, rather stroppily, "we didn't ask you to include optional brain plug-ins, did we? You computed that all by yourself."

Why was she so cross? I didn't see the problem.

"YOU DIDN'T *NOT* ASK ME EITHER," replied Russell.

"Ha," said Bird. "So we have to tell you what we don't want, as well as what we do want?"

"YES," said Russell. "I MAKE THINGS TO THE BEST OF MY ABILITY. IT'S LOGICAL TO INCLUDE OPTIONAL BRAIN PLUG-INS ON A HUMANOID STRUCTURE. THE BRAIN IS THE ESSENCE OF HUMAN."

"Not in my case," admitted Stevie, who had yet to master his five times tables.

"What else is it 'logical' to include?" demanded Bird. "Would you, for example, include optional mobility attachments?"

"What's that?" whispered Stevie.

"So that he might be able to walk one day," I replied.

"I ALREADY HAVE THAT PLANNED," admitted Russell. "I HEARD YOU MENTION ANIMATRONICS."

"What's that?" whispered Stevie.

"Music from other countries?" I suggested uncertainly.

"No," said Bird. "Animatronics is the technique for making motorized puppets."

"Ah," said Stevie, giving me the Long Look.

I don't understand either, I thought-spoke back.

"YOU ARE AN INTELLIGENT CHILD," said Russell. (He definitely wasn't talking to me or Stevie.)

"I know," said Bird. "Watch out." She unbolted the door and swept out of the Mob. "I'm going to look some stuff up on the internet."

"What stuff?" called Stevie.

"Robotic ethics."

Neither of us knew what that meant, but we were used to not understanding a large proportion of what our sister was saying so we just forgot about it.

"The ears are perfect," said Stevie, pinging one.

"It's freaky," I said.

"DO YOU WANT ME TO PRINT THE CHEST?" asked Russell.

"Go for it," I said.

And off Russell went, whirring away, the fat, electronic needle swooping back and forth along the production plate, which sank lower and lower as the body grew on it. We watched, mesmerized, and then Stevie sniggered.

"He's naked," he said.

Russell huffed. "OF COURSE HE IS NAKED. WHY WOULD I PRINT CLOTHES? IT WOULD BE A VERY INEFFICIENT USE OF TIME AND RESOURCES."

"There's still a box of Dad's clothes in the attic," I said. "We can dress him in those."

"But what happens when we print his bum?" whispered Stevie. "Will we see his willy?"

"It won't be a real willy, it will be a plastic one," I said.

"I CAN LEAVE OUT THE WILLY, IF YOU WANT," said Russell. "HE WON'T MIND."

"I'd always mind not having a willy," said Stevie.

"This is getting weird," I said. So I popped back into the house to find the clothes.

Mum was unloading the dishwasher and saying, "Hey there, Mrs Bear" in a daft, growly voice to the baby.

Ella was cracking up like it was the funniest thing ever.

"Do you think I should make some knickers that go *down the leg?*" asked Mum, looking up. "You know, to slim the thigh?"

"Do I look like an expert on women's pants?" I said, somewhat huffily.

"You smell funny," said Mum.

"Not as bad as her," I said, pointing at Ella, who looked guilty.

"But what designs should the knickers have?" mused Mum. "Floral? Sporty?" She frowned. "Is Bird out there with you?"

"Sort of."

"What are you doing?"

"This and that," I said.

"I know. The eternal school project. You're not setting fire to anything, are you?"

Mum's from an era when the worst things kids could do was set fire to things (which is still very bad) and run off and hide in barns. Stuff like that. Consequently she usually has no idea what we are up to. It's kind of fun.

I shifted to the other foot. "I need to get something

from the attic. Do you mind if I get the ladder down?"

"Go ahead," said Mum. "I wouldn't want to get in the way of the school project. Are you sure about the long knickers? Do you think they'll want tummy control?"

I backed out of the room. "PLEASE, MUM. NOT MY THING."

I found the box of clothes under a pile of old coats. I opened the cardboard lid and picked up some trousers, a blue shirt, some red socks and some pants. There was also one of Dad's jumpers. It was dark blue with a criss-cross design. He used to wear it a lot. It was so much HIM that I felt a wobble in my tummy and my eyeballs felt wet. Why hadn't our dad collected it? Maybe it was a sign that eventually he would come back.

I hope you understand that Dad is not the "baddie" of this story. OK, he left his wife and four children nine weeks ago and he's only called us twice, but HE IS NOT THE BADDIE. OK?

He and Mum were arguing loads and loads, worse than me and Stevie, and then one night he just left. I thought Mum would go crazy, but she didn't. She said it was time to start having some fun. Looking after all of us must be lots of fun.

I took everything downstairs and snuck them out of the door before Mum could see. I didn't want any awkward questions.

Bird had already come back when I returned. She barely looked at the clothes, as she was busy with Stevie, printing out Dad's torso. It needed lots and lots of cartridges of plastic stringy stuff and she had to keep adding the right amount of colouring to turn his skin the right shade.

There was a hitch when Dad's torso was nearly finished. We had a power cut and Russell did a loud BLEEP.

"What's up, Russ?" asked Stevie as the lights went out.

"POWER SHUTDOWN. I WILL NOT TALK TO CONSERVE ENERGY. I AM ON MY BACK-UP BATTERY," said Russell. A black panel the length of my leg eased out of him and tilted towards the light.

"Solar," said Bird approvingly. "Very good."

And Russell valiantly carried on printing.

"I'll go check the trip switch," said Bird.

Bird, as I have already explained, was good at trip switches and a zillion other useful things like that. Her eyes gleamed, like a cat watching a butterfly, when something technical went wrong.

Two minutes later, the lights came back on and Russell beeped again. The printing never faltered.

When it was finished, the torso was slightly warm and smelled of plastic bags. Russell had cunningly left a couple of grooves in his neck. All we had to do was slot it together.

We put the shirt on him straight away, even though he didn't have any arms or legs yet, because it didn't seem very kind to leave him naked when it was a bit chilly.

"Ha ha!" giggled Stevie, pointing. Russell had printed a sort-of willy, like tube of Smarties, in the pants area.

"YOU ARE VERY CHILDISH," said Russell sniffily.

"It's my job," protested Stevie. "Don't worry, I won't be a child for ever."

*

At bedtime we left Russell still printing. He said he would make the frame or skeleton of Dad overnight and that we would have to assemble the rest around that. Russell was using this composite metal powder, which Bird said would make a very strong frame, much stronger than real bones.

Bird said she would stay on for a bit and keep an eye on things. She doesn't have to go to bed until ten o'clock, the lucky thing. I hate bedtime. It always ambushes us just when the best bits of the day are happening.

When we came inside, Mum looked really tired and a bit sad and red around the eyes.

"Can I come and see what you've been doing?" she asked. "I haven't seen you all day."

"Top secret," said Stevie. "Can I play MAZZO before bed?"

chapters[16].title =

"Space Puppies";

On Sunday morning Bird came in to breakfast from outside with a pleased expression on her face. She was wearing the same clothes (a silver T-shirt and red jeans) that she'd been wearing the night before. She also had the same, now extremely scruffy, bun in her hair. This got me wondering if she had been to bed at all.

Mum was obviously wondering the same thing.

"Why have you just come out of the Mob at eight in the morning?"

"Me and the boys are compiling a giant robot," said Bird coolly. "I wanted to see how he was doing."

"Ha ha." Mum raised her eyes to the ceiling. She was in her pyjamas, her hair was all over the place and she was wearing odd socks. She had big rings around her eyes and there was dried baby sick on her shoulder. Mum usually looks OK, but this morning she looked pretty bad. This is probably because Ella is a baby and everyone knows babies are creatures of the night, so Mum was always extremely tired.

"Last night I dreamed I went to bed," she murmured. "It was a nice dream."

"MUM," said Stevie, putting down his MAZZO manual. "Go and have a shower. We will clear up and look after Ella."

Most little brothers (including Stevie) are annoying, but I have to admit, he does know how to be kind.

"Yes, go," said Bird. She was not kind like Stevie – she probably had a twisty reason for wanting Mum out the way – but Mum leaped at the chance like she was the jumper in a line-out.

"My dream children," said Mum. In seconds she had winged the baby to me and belted up the stairs before Ella even noticed she'd gone.

"What are you up to?" I asked Bird, as Ella grinned goofily at me.

Bird looked shifty. "A few modifications," she said. She dolloped some of Mum's legendarily solid porridge into a bowl.

I felt a surge of annoyance.

"What sort of modifications?"

"Exciting ones." said Bird, chewing on the porridge. She stood and picked up her bowl.

"I've been up all night," she whispered, "working on the skeleton-frame with Russell."

"I thought you didn't trust him," I said.

"I don't," said Bird. "But it's been such fun. It's going better than I could have dreamed." She grinned, looking happier than I'd seen her for weeks. Her phone trilled the tune "Life on Mars" by David Bowie. This meant her almost-boyfriend, Iqbal, was calling her. Like Bird, Iqbal was a bit of a know-it-all, though I know for a fact he is quite effective in goal. But Bird just switched the phone off.

"You're not going to tell Iqbal about all this?" I asked cautiously. (*No, no, please no*, I thought.)

"Of course not," said Bird. "I'm not having him butting in. This is MY thing." She caught my eye. "Our thing," she amended. She headed for the door. "Now, whatever you do, don't let Mum in the Mob."

I knew this would happen. I knew my sister would take over. But what could I do?

I fled out of the house and into the Mob and – *wham!* – the blinking nail gored my arm again.

"Ow, ow, ow," I yelped, though I soon forgot about it, because Dad now had two legs and it was *all attached!*

"I wanted to build Dad," I protested.

"Forget it, it's not Lego," said Bird meanly.

"What have you done to him?" I asked.

Dad looked different to last night. He was much more *real*. The shape of his back and the curve of his neck, the way his ears poked out. Looking at him made me feel sad and odd.

"Inspect," said Bird, and she gently manipulated his head so it turned like a real head. Then she showed me his bendy toes and locking knees. "We printed the skeleton. I had to screw so many little bits together." She yawned. "Now, very sadly, I have to go and do my homework. I'm going to trust you to print his arms down to his wrist. Russell will talk you through it. Leave the fingers to me."

"You don't have to TRUST me to do anything," I snapped. "This is MY machine. I'm only letting you in on this because I want to." I examined my arm where the nail had got me. It was quite a deep cut.

"Yadda, yadda," slurred Bird. "You need me, Olly. You couldn't have done this on your own."

I shut my mouth. It was true. I wanted to flick a bogey-ball at her, though.

"ARE YOU READY, OLLY?" asked Russell, as Bird departed.

"I suppose so." I was feeling miffed that loads of printing had happened without me.

"EXCELLENT. FILL HOPPER D WITH RESIN POWDER 642…"

And so it went on.

After exactly one hour, Stevie joined me, fresh from MAZZO.

"I've got three new Space Puppies," he beamed. "They are so cute. The Queen came to see them and awarded me twenty lob-bombs and fifty oxygen points. The puppies are called Gary, Larry and Carrie."

"Cool," I said.

We squeezed into the armchair together and watched the machine move back and forth over the production plate, gradually producing a hairless, hollow forearm.

"Mum nearly came out with me," Stevie mentioned. "She's going mad with desperation and nosiness about what we are doing."

"How did you stop her?" I asked, alarmed.

"Bird said we were making her something for her birthday."

I didn't like all this lying. Mum didn't deserve it.

"We could always GIVE her the new Dad for her birthday," said Stevie. "Then it wouldn't be a lie."

"Bad idea," I said. Mum and Dad had argued A LOT in the weeks before Dad left. Why would she want a copy of someone she obviously didn't like? That thought made my throat feel tight and my head swim. I did a few MAZZO low atmosphere muscle-building exercises to distract me from myself.

"What is Bird doing anyway?" I asked.

"Researching weird stuff on the internet," said Stevie.

I knew she wasn't doing her homework.

By Sunday evening we'd nearly finished. All we had to do was Dad's left foot. We'd had to come in the house and mess around and act like children, though, because Mum was getting jumpy. Me and Stevie even pretended to have a fight, just to look authentic.

"Hello, strangers," Mum said. "I hear you are making me a present."

"Hmmm," I grunted, because Stevie was sitting on my head and my face was flattened.

"What have you done to your arm?" (I was trying to drag Stevie off me.)

"Nail," I gasped. "It's fine." I tipped Stevie on to the carpet and swerved to avoid a foot lashing as Bird appeared on the stairs. She was wearing her Headsetz.

"The Futures Project intergalactic ship is nearly finished."

She was talking about MAZZO, of course. She,

too, could not leave it alone, even when she was in the middle of this crazy Dad-bot business.

"Cool, can I see?" said Stevie, getting up.

"No, it's top secret," said Bird.

Bird was also pretty important in the world of MAZZO. Her avatar was this mad MAZZO scientist. She spent her MAZZO time in the Futures Project lab with all the other scientists. We rarely saw her in our games.

"I thought you were doing homework," said Mum.

"MAZZO was my homework," said Bird. "I had to produce some code to replicate a new MAZZO world."

"Let me find you a plaster for that arm." Mum dumped Ella in my arms and went off to the bathroom cabinet.

Ella looked at me and grinned. I only have to pull a stupid face and she creases up with her mad baby laughing.

When Mum was out of earshot, Bird leaned forward, a serious look on her face

"I've decided I'm going to lock the Mob," she said. "I don't want anyone snooping around and getting in."

"Like who?" I asked. I felt annoyed. This was my thing after all.

"Like Mum," said Bird. "Or the people who actually own Russell."

We went a bit quiet. I had come to think of Russell as mine. Even though we'd only had him for a few days. Ella gently bit my nose and chuckled.

"But we also need to keep it locked," Bird took Ella from me and lowered her voice so much I could barely hear her, *to stop things from getting out.*

chapters[17].title =
"The Drone";

It's hard to concentrate at school when you've nearly made your dad.

On Monday I missed three easy goals in lunchtime football practice and I got only two out of twenty in my spelling test and I couldn't answer when my teacher, Mrs McCurdy, asked me a question about a book I'd read last week.

"What made you like the book?"

I should have been able to answer because I'd written a book review on why I'd liked it. But when she asked me, my mind went holey and I couldn't remember one single thing.

I kept wondering what Russell was doing. I knew he was turned off at the plug, but I'd been impressed by the way his solar panel slid out during the power cut.

What if it was sliding out right now?

What if Russell decided to start making something all by himself? He struck me as being that sort of machine. He was a bit wild, for a printer. Like him including those brain plug-ins. Why had he done that?

"Olly?"

I blinked.

The whole class was silent, and, I realized, were staring at me. So was Mrs McCurdy.

Rats.

I fell back on a trick Bird had taught me. *The secret of school survival for dreamers.*

"Please could you repeat the question?" I asked innocently.

Mrs McCurdy's eyes grew slitty and suspicious, but luckily Frances Belter was whispering to Evie Smith so Mrs McCurdy had to wade in and shut them up.

Phew.

"Olly!"

Mrs McCurdy folded her arms and twisted her lips.

"You need to focus or you'll miss out on vital information."

"OK," I said.

"You need to stop rushing off on tangents."

"What's a tangent?" asked Susie.

"It's a kind of orange you only get at Christmas," said Fred.

"Oranges are nutritious," said Susie, shooting a swotty look at Mrs McCurdy.

"Can we come and swim in your pool?" asked Fred.

"No. There is no pool," I said.

"There's only five minutes until break," said Mrs McCurdy weakly. "Shall we play hangman?"

At break I was kicking a football around with Joe and Raz, when Henrietta Stibbens came gunning up to me.

"Where'd your little brother get the Space Hound?" she demanded.

"Amazon," I replied quickly.

"I knew he was lying," said Henrietta. "Stevie said you PRINTED it, with a 3D printer, like the sweets and the pool."

I watched as she stalked away. Then a football hit me in the head and I decided not to worry about things I couldn't control. Like Henrietta Stibbens.

When I got home, the place was empty. There was note from Mum saying she was at the Bloomers unit with Ella. Stevie had got astronaut club.

Bird doesn't get home until four. I was just about to fire off and check the Mob when I caught sight of my phone and decided to have a few sneaky moments on MAZZO.

My avatar lives in a little brown bubble house. It's made of dust and red rocks. It's basic, but it is safe. No one can throw a lob-bomb at me or send in gases. Orsps cannot come in unless I let them. My brother and sister's places are very different to mine. Stevie lives in the Royal Kennels and Bird lives in the Science Lab.

I heard a whining noise coming from outside, like

a giant wasp, and I put my head round the door to investigate.

The drone was back, but it was lower than it had ever been before – only about three metres above my head. It buzzed up and down, a blue light winking on and off. The black lens glinted in the sun like a giant eye.

I made a rude sign at it. I knew this was bad, but I couldn't stop myself. Nobody invited this thing into my garden. It was trespassing. And if it was going to be rude then I could be rude back.

"Go away," I said. "I hate you."

It whizzed up over the swing and hovered over Mum's overgrown veggie patch. Suddenly it swooped, like it was a buzzard and I was a mouse. It was coming straight at my head. I let out a little yelp and covered my face with my hands.

But then the drone rose straight up into the air, climbing steadily, up and up, past the eaves of the house and beyond the roof.

I think it must belong to some nosy kid with nothing better to do.

The back gate crashed open and Bird stepped in, dropping her bag on the floor and kicking off her shoes.

"So Olly. Shall we do it? Shall we try and finish Dad?" she said. "Or should we stop now, in case…"

"In case what?" I asked. "Of course we've got to finish him."

chapters[18].title =
"The Dad-Bot";

"DONE!" announced Russell.

A perfect left foot revolved on the production plate.

"That's the last bit," said Bird. She was being a bit weird and quiet. "Shall we fix it on now or wait for Stevie?"

"But then Mum will be back too. Let's just do it." I carried the foot over to the rest of the Dad-bot. He was sitting on my armchair and dressed in one of Dad's shirts and a pair of jogging bottoms. The foot slotted on to the ankle stump so perfectly I couldn't see the join.

Holding her breath, Bird put her hand on my shoulder as Russell's lens swivelled round to look.

"DOES HE RESEMBLE YOUR FATHER?"

The Dad-bot sat motionless. His arms were folded and his hands had the same wrinkles and moles as Dad's. His hair was tousled to one side like Dad's and his facial expression was amused and a bit distracted.

"Yes," I said.

"No," said Bird.

The door of the Mob flew open and Bird automatically jumped in front of the Dad-bot, but it was only Stevie.

"Henrietta Stibbens chucked up, so we all came home early. WHOOOOAAAAAAA." Stevie skidded to a halt. "Check him out!" He stood open-mouthed, staring.

"WHAT IS WRONG WITH HIM? WHAT IS MISSING? I CAN PRINT ANYTHING," said Russell.

Bird hesitated. "It's the sparkle of life in his eyes. It will activate him. It's the last step in the program I made."

"I DON'T KNOW IF I CAN PRINT THAT." Russell rumbled and there was a smell of hot metal. "BUT I WILL TRY."

The needle started whizzing up and down. In just a few seconds, two little silver crescents lay glittering on the production plate.

"PLACE THEM ON HIS EYES," said Russell.

As I reached out for them, Bird put her hand on my arm. "NO," she said. "Wait."

"Why?"

"I don't know. I feel a bit scared. On Saturday night we put a lot of extra machinery inside." She paused. "An awful lot. I got carried away. I never thought I could do this. I didn't believe I could create a real, animated robot to such detail. But I think I have... I —

There was a clicking noise behind us and, to my utter amazement, the Dad-Bot unfolded his arms and stretched. His synthetic lips broke into an awful grin. Awful, because he was so like Dad, and yet so unlike Dad. We watched, stunned, as he unfurled his fingers one by one. He blew out his cheeks and turned his head smoothly to look at us.

"Nice work," said Bird in a small voice.

"THANKS," said Russell. "I COULDN'T HAVE DONE IT WITHOUT YOU."

There was so much I wanted to say, like, "Bird! WHAT THE HECK HAVE YOU DONE?" But I was mesmerized by the thing we had made.

The Dad-bot rose to his feet and walked over to Russell. He picked up the silver sparks and pressed them into his own eyes.

Then he moved his head round and looked at us.

"Hi," he said.

The Dad-bot shook each of our hands in turn. His fingers felt soft and squishy. Bird, who was very twitchy, kept her hands behind her back.

"You're not collecting any data from me," she whispered.

"What do you mean?" asked Stevie, who had gone all shy, because this bloke looked JUST LIKE OUR DAD, but he wasn't, and that was confusing.

"This machine might be after our DNA."

"Why would he do that?"

"I don't know," said Bird. "But I'm not giving him the option of future mischief with my DNA." She groaned. "What have I done?"

"Bird," I said nervously. "One minute this robot thing is all you can think about, it was your idea for crikey's sake. Now you are freaking out. What's going on?"

"I'm a scientist," grimaced Bird. "Sometimes I just get way too swept up in my experiments to consider the consequences." She paused. "Like Victor Frankenstein."

The Dad-bot squatted next to me.

AMAZING! He looked so real!

"Now I am looking at those consequences," whispered Bird to herself. "Wow, I am way more clever than I thought."

"I'm sorry I'm not your dad," the robot said. His voice was absolutely NOT Dad's. He sounded like someone standing behind a door. He smiled. I watched and his lips really parted and his teeth peeked through. The teeth were the right shape but way too bright. His smile was all wrong because he only moved his mouth.

"If you want me to be like your dad, you have to tell me all about him," he said. **"I need information. Where was he born? Did he have brothers or sisters? What were his hobbies as a child? When did he marry your mother? Where did he propose?"**

"Slow down," said Stevie. "That's a lot to answer."

"How can you speak so well?" asked Bird. "I didn't fit a voice box or include a vocabulary chip."

"I DID," said Russell. "SILENT ROBOTS ARE TOO SCARY. YOU DON'T KNOW WHAT THEY ARE THINKING."

"I need much more information to become their father," said the Dad-bot.

Russell *ahem*'ed. "YOU ARE JUST AN IMAGE, NOT A TRUE COPY."

"I don't want to be just an image," said the Dad-bot. **"I want to be perfect!"**

"YOU WILL NEVER BE PERFECT," said Russell.

"Then I'll have to make myself perfect," said the Dad-bot.

"I knew I should have stopped myself," muttered Bird. "But it was just TOO exciting."

Stevie looked as puzzled as I felt. Here we were, in our Mob, watching two machines having an argument.

The Dad-bot turned to Bird. **"Take me to your home computer."**

"Negative," said Bird.

"Why does he want a computer? We've got Russell here – he's attached to the internet."

"I've got all I want from him," said the Dad-bot.

"OH, DEAR," said Russell.

"I need details. I can build a personal history by looking at all your family photographs on your computer. I want to be authentic," said the Dad-bot.

"Slow down," I said.

Bird took me by the arm and led me and Stevie out of the Mob and under the rhubarb.

"This has got *reallllllly* confusing," she whispered. "This guy, he is probably fine, but he could be dangerous. He could hurt us."

"Bird, my sister," I replied, "you love technology.

You helped build this guy. You are always telling us we have no thirst for progress. Why are you saying this?"

"We need to get rid of him now," said Bird. "The experiment is over. Phone the police."

```
chapters[19].title =
```

"The Dad—Bot Goes Away";

But we did not phone the police. We all went inside (after telling the Dad-bot he REALLY HAD to stay in the Mob) and played with the baby, messed around with Piggy, played MAZZO and ate tea (spaghetti bolognese) as if nothing had happened.

In MAZZO, I updated my avatar so he was wearing a red jumper. I spent my hour exploring the empty Orsp craters on the other side of the planet.

Me and Stevie had conducted a silent conversation and we'd decided to wait and see what Bird did about the Dad-bot After all, she'd spent most of Saturday night building him, so she knew more about any potential problems than us. I just wanted to go out and stare at him but I did not want to arouse Mum's suspicion by NOT playing MAZZO.

"School trouble?" Mum scrutinized her eldest daughter. "How's Iqbal? We haven't seen him lately."

"Everything's fine," said Bird, casually forking a heap of spaghetti.

I wondered why Bird hadn't told Mum about the Dad-bot if she was so worried about it/him.

Should I call Dad bot "it" or "him"? He obviously isn't a real "him" but he is a VERSION of a real "him". So does that make him a "him"? Or is he just an "it"? When does an "it" become a "him"?

Later, when Mum was lost in some work emails, I took Bird aside.

"What about HIM?" I said. "Aren't you worried he is going to turn bad and hurt us any more?"

"Nope," said Bird. "'Cos I saw him leave about two hours ago."

chapters[20].title =

"The Dad–Bot Comes Back";

As we huddled under the giant rhubarb, Bird told us what she had seen. Just before tea she'd gone upstairs and looked out of her window. The Mob door had opened, the Dad-bot had stepped out, walked calmly to the end of the garden, slid through the rhubarb and hopped over the fence. One of the thick, prickly rhubarb stalks was a bit crushed where he must have pushed through.

"Why didn't you tell us?" I said, outraged.

"I couldn't say anything in front of Mum," replied Bird. "And I thought you guys might try and bring him back."

"But where is he?" asked Stevie. "I thought you'd locked the Mob."

"I must have forgotten," shrugged Bird, in a way that made me think she'd left it open on purpose.

Bird smiled. "So now, he's somewhere else, that's all that matters. I hope he never comes back."

"You're mad," said Stevie. "We've spent DAYS building this guy and now you don't want him."

I was struggling with a thought that I didn't want to think, but I couldn't help it. Mum would have said it was my conscience.

"If you think the Dad-bot is dangerous, shouldn't we stop him going out in the world?"

Bird nodded. "He'll run out of energy soon."

This was a relief to hear.

"So someone will just find him lying in the street?" asked Stevie. "That will be weird for them."

"Maybe we'll never see him again," said Bird.

I felt sad about that. I'd printed pretend-Dad because I missed our real dad. Now even the pretend one had gone.

I've already told you that before Dad got the sack he'd travelled a lot, all over Europe, doing his engineering projects. He was often away for two weeks at a time. So we are very used to NOT having him around. But since he left us, it's like there is a Dad-shaped space in the air, and the Dad-bot did fill in that empty space, just a tiny, tiny bit.

I looked at Bird.

"I still don't understand why you are so negative about him, when he was all your idea."

"Lots of scientists have bad ideas," said Bird grimly. "Look at Rutherford when he split the atom."

I wasn't sure what she was talking about (no change there) but it didn't sound very good.

"Lots of scientific experiments turn out good," I said, trying to keep pace with her. "Like the bloke who discovered Pencilwomen."

"You mean penicillin," said Bird. "The problem is, you don't really know what the outcome will be until it's too late."

She looked at me meaningfully before vanishing upstairs to her lair.

*

We were uneasily watching evening TV when someone detonated the doorbell.

I went to the door and opened it.

I gasped. Because for a half of split second, I thought he was real.

"Hello," said the Dad-bot. **"I'm back."**

Aunty Vi, our cat, had come to answer the door with me and when she saw the robot she arched her back and hissed, her tail growing fat and bristly.

I couldn't help feeling pleased. I knew Bird was worried, but I didn't see why. What would be the point of the Dad-bot hurting us?

I smuggled the Dad-bot in through the hallway, straight through the kitchen and out of the back door, hoping Mum wouldn't look out of the bathroom window, where she was giving Ella a bath. The Dad-bot ran as well as he walked. The only thing I thought that might give him away was that he moved TOO smoothly. Most people have a bit of a swagger or a limp, or stop and start, or a shuffle or something. Stevie has a habit of going on his tiptoes when he's excited and

Bird taps her feet when sitting and has a really bouncy walk.

The Dad-bot had nothing like this.

Safely in the Mob, he turned to face me.

"Sorry I went away," he said. **"I just wanted a look around."**

I wondered if any of our neighbours had seen him.

"HELLO!" said Russell, twinkling into life, or artificial life anyway. "YOU ARE BACK!"

The Dad-bot ignored him. The way he snubbed him reminded me of how the cool kids at school don't talk to the uncool kids. I felt sorry for Russell. Next to the Dad-bot, Russell definitely did not look cool. The Dad-bot had legs and arms and silver lights in his eyes. He looked like a mad superhero. A very handsome, souped-up version of my dad. Poor Russell was like a giant sewing machine.

"I am ready," announced the Dad-bot.

"Ready for what?" I asked nervously. Was he going to start trying to take over the world?

Bird and Stevie burst in.

"Hurrah!" said Stevie, pleased.

"Oh, no," said Bird, displeased.

"I am ready," repeated the Dad-bot.

"I know," I replied. "But what for?"

"Give me my orders, my reason for being created. I need something to do," said the Dad-bot.

"We can't code properly," said Stevie. "We don't get taught until Year Eight."

"Bird can code," I said.

"I can code, yes, but I don't know what language to code him in," said Bird.

"You code me by talking to me," said the Dad-bot. **"Codes are old-fashioned. Let's speak English."**

"So our voices are like the source code?" asked Bird.

Russell blinked and whistled. "YOUR VOICES MUST IMPRINT THEMSELVES ON ME. THEN THIS ITEM CAN BE PROGRAMMED," Russell announced.

"What was that?" asked Stevie.

"We need to program him through Russell," said Bird.

"No, you don't," said the Dad-bot.

"YES, YOU DO," said Russell. "IT IS IN YOUR DESIGN. I AM IN CHARGE OF YOU."

We all felt comforted by that.

"You are not in charge of me," said the Dad-bot matter-of-factly. **"I overrode that preference."**

Russell went very still, as if he was thinking deeply. (Though, of course, he wasn't. Because machines can't think deeply, can they?)

"IF YOU OVERRODE THE DOCKING TO THE MOTHERLODE YOU WOULD NEED TO HAVE OVERRIDDEN THE ENERGY CORE, THE INTERNET SCREENING AND PASSWORDS. YOU WOULD HAVE OVERRIDDEN THE LOCK CONCERNING YOUR BLUEPRINT AND YOUR ETHICAL LIMITATIONS."

"Correct," said the Dad-bot.

"OH, DEAR," said Russell.

"What's Russell on about now?" asked Stevie.

Bird had gone quiet. "It means the Dad-bot can do what he likes. Russell has no control over him."

"Well, we have no control over Russell, so what's the difference?" I said reasonably.

"It means the Dad-bot is making decisions off his own bat," said Bird. She rubbed her nose anxiously. "It's almost as if he is sentient."

She was, I noticed, very like our real dad at that moment, with a faraway look in her eyes.

"OH, DEAR," said Russell. "THIS MEANS I WILL HAVE TO DESTROY YOU."

We all went quiet. I didn't like the idea of anyone or anything destroying anything.

"You can't," said the Dad-bot firmly. **"No more talk, let's have some action. PROGRAM ME! I need a job! Give me my algorithm!"**

Bird chewed her thumbnail.

"I'd like you to just stay in here and do nothing."

"I can't compute nothing," said Dad-bot. **"I cannot think of anything that is nothing."**

chapters[21].title =

"The First Order";

But there was something I wanted to sort out first.

"You need a name," I said. "'Dad-bot' sounds like 'Dad-bottom'."

Stevie sniggered.

"What was your father called?" asked the Dad-bot.

"He shouldn't have Dad's name." Bird seemed to slump. "It's no use pretending he is anything like him."

"Dad IS called Oscar," said Stevie. "And this guy is A LOT like him."

"Idiot," said Bird.

"'Oscar-Idiot'? I would not like to be called

.hat," said the Dad-bot, which made us all smile, even Bird.

"How about Chip!" she suggested, perking up. "Or Sparky."

"Mister Robot Man," said Stevie.

"Mister Rob," I said. "Or Mister for short."

And so he was named.

"Give me my orders," said Mister Rob.

"That's it?"

"Yes," said Mister Rob.

Bird sniffed. "We need to have a talk," she said, and led us all outside to the giant rhubarb.

From the house we could hear Mum singing to Ella.

"We have to be careful when we give him his orders."

"Why?" asked Stevie, scratching his nose.

"Because he might get it wrong. What did you want him to do, Olly?"

I tried to think. I hadn't yet decided. What I really wanted him to do was play football with me, but I felt a bit shy to say this.

"I want him to do Dad things."

"Way too vague," said Bird. "He needs precise directions. Don't say anything that could be misinterpreted."

"Sure," said Stevie.

Bird's windmill was making a squeaking noise so she went to investigate.

Stevie thought-spoke to me.

What does misinterpreted mean?

It means the thing when you are NOT interrupted, I replied confidently.

Oh, right, said Stevie, looking thoughtful. *Like not saying when you don't believe someone?*

Yup, I said. *Definitely, probably. Actually, don't ask me.*

And Stevie went in for a sliding tackle against me even though I didn't have a ball.

So I was lying face down, with a mouthful of grass, when the Mob door creaked open. Just for a moment my heart seemed to stop. The shape of Mister Rob's head and the curve of his nose were so like Dad's. Also the set of his shoulders. I had to sit up and swallow hard to stop myself getting miserable.

Then he spoke and he sounded so unlike Dad.

"Are you ready?" he asked.

"I've got it," said Stevie, all fired up from his victory flooring me. "Can you clear up my room? I'd like everything sorted out and looking really tidy."

"Of course," said Mister.

"That's sooooo boring," I said.

Stevie stuck out his tongue. "I know, but Mum said I couldn't go on MAZZO until it was done."

Bird belted back from her windmill. "Did you give him clear instructions?" she asked anxiously.

"Yep," said Stevie. "Just to sort out my room."

"When would you like me to begin?" asked Mister Rob.

"Now, please," said Stevie.

"Which is your room?"

Stevie pointed to the left hand back window, where MAZZO Orsp sticker clung to the glass.

Mister Rob started off towards the house.

"Hang on. What about Mum?" Bird called. "She'll see you!"

Mister Rob halted and turned his head. He really did

look *almost* human. **"You wish to pretend YOU cleared up the room?"** he said to Stevie.

"YES."

Mister Rob stuck both his thumbs up, the tip of the left one twitching quicker than humanly possible. He paused, leaned back, and did a mighty leap, landing at the wall of the house. As we watched, he deftly climbed the drainpipe, as agile as a giant hairless squirrel. He tugged open Stevie's bedroom window and slipped over the sill.

"Wow," I said. "Dad can't do that."

"Why do I have a bad feeling about this?" asked Bird. "What have we unleashed?"

"He can do much more that I thought," I said.

"Me too," said Bird. "I think he's somehow updating himself, all the time. I hadn't programmed in a climb factor or inputted non-verbal communication, like those thumbs-up. He's done that himself."

"Or Russell is a rogue 3D printer and did it all behind our backs," I said jokingly.

Bird did not smile.

```
chapters[22].title =
```

"Mister Rob Clears Up";

Mum was sitting cross-legged on the floor of our little sitting room, surrounded by boxes of knickers and photo albums. This morning, a new type of Bloomers pants had arrived. These pants apparently came up to your armpits and Mum had been very excited about them, but now she was looking through old photo albums and completely ignoring them.

"Look," she said, smiling.

There was a photo of Dad with Bird as a baby. They were both holding massive red leaves and grinning like fools. Dad had a bizarre beard and a green checked scarf.

"GNNARRRR," said Ella, who had got into the pants box and was wearing a spotty pair on her head. She offered some to me and smiled encouragingly, so I put them on my head too.

"Heh heh," said Ella.

Mum didn't notice, she was so engrossed.

The next photo was me and Bird, aged about five and seven, when we'd taken the broken TV apart for fun. It was an old box TV, big and heavy, and inside were all sorts of colourful components and circuits and electrical bits and pieces. There was a big glass tank too, which Bird had tried to turn into an aquarium. The TV sat full of water for about a month before it started to smell and Dad took it away.

"I miss Dad," I said.

I don't know why I said that. The words just came out before I had even thought them.

Mum hugged me. "I know."

There was a loud crash from upstairs.

We ignored it. In a house with this many children, there are always thumps and bangs and moans and yowling.

"Look, it's you holding baby Stevie." Mum pointed. "You were so amazed when we brought him home, you kept going over to his cot to check he was real."

As she went on I noticed the fringe around the lampshade was vibrating. Also another box, full of Bloomers pants, was wobbling on the sideboard. There were clanging and whirring sounds coming through the floorboards. Mum carried on, oblivious. "Look at your CUTE little face!"

Then there was a grinding noise, like a food processor going off and on and off and on. What was Mister Rob doing up there?

BANG!

"Look, your first tooth!" said Mum. "Do stop tapping, Olly."

I realized I had been drumming the floor with my fists. It must be nerves.

"Wales!" said Mum, turning over a page. "The year me and your dad stayed in the cottage without any of you children. We ate a massive meal and I slept for twenty-four hours."

"You look happy," I said, touching the photo.

"I was," said Mum, and sighed.

There was the sound of smashing glass. I definitely felt twitchy now.

"Halloween last year!" said Mum, brandishing yet another photo. "Remember, you all dressed as Orsps."

THUMP!

"What's Stevie up to?" asked Mum, finally roused from her trip down memory lane.

"Tidying his room," I said, grimacing at a violent clatter.

Mum's face clouded. "Really? That's odd."

"Well, you did ask him to," I said.

BANG!!

More squealing, crunching and grinding noises.

"He sounds like he's got power tools up there." Mum reluctantly started to get up.

"I'll see if he needs a hand," I said, passing her the baby.

I met Stevie hovering on the stairs.

"He's wedged the door shut," he whispered. "I hope he hasn't broken anything."

The door swung open and Mister Rob strode out, patting dust from his clothes. Unidentifiable flecks, like fish food, speckled his hair.

"All cleared up." He smiled his awful, bright smile.

As we stepped into the room a thick cloud of yellow dust blew into our faces.

"OH NO," gasped Stevie.

There was no bed, no table, no chair. There was no cupboard and no clothes. The carpet had gone. Even the wallpaper had been stripped down to the plaster. The curtains were missing. There was nothing left. Stevie's stereo, his TV, his clothes, posters and books, were all gone.

"Where is everything?" whispered Stevie.

"All cleared up, like you asked," said Mister Rob. "I will recycle these shortly." He pointed to five piles in the corner of the room.

One pile contained silver beads of glass, the next, crumbs of plastic. There were also piles of material fragments, shredded paper and, finally, a glinting heap of metal slithers of all colours.

"But, but, I didn't mean clear up THIS MUCH,"

squeaked Stevie. "Where's all my stuff? Where's my mammoth duvet and my fake tusk? Where are my binoculars?"

"There." Mister Rob pointed to the piles. **"Do you want me to clear up anything else?"**

"Noooooo!" we yelled.

Then poor Stevie, fingering a shred of furry wool, burst into tears.

"NO!" he sobbed. "This is from Stinky Elephant. He's KILLED Stinky Elephant."

"Is he sad?" asked Mister, puzzled.

"Very," I replied, and gave my brother's shoulders a squeeze. "He didn't want you to clear up this much."

"He should have specified," said Mister Rob.

We heard footsteps on the stairs.

"Is everything all right?"

"It's Mum," sniffed Stevie tearfully. "What do we do?"

It was a tricky one to be sure.

"I must hide," said Mister. **"You don't want her to see me."** Without hesitation, he pushed open the window and sprang out.

We waited for the crash landing, but there was none, only the sound of Mum coming closer.

I hustled Stevie out of his room. "We can't let her see, she'll go crazy." I felt fairly crazy myself. It was hard to believe what I had seen. How had Mister Rob done it? I had no idea he was so powerful.

"Hey, guys," said Mum, climbing the stairs with baby Ella. "I've been investigating the competition. I've found this other company that makes reinforced ladies knickers so I've just bought three pairs to discover their secrets." She noticed the tears shining on my brother's cheeks. "Stevie, what's wrong?"

chapters[23].title =

"The Return of the Drone";

We managed to get Mum downstairs before she saw Stevie's room. But it was only a matter of seconds, minutes, hours or days before she found out the awful truth.

I bravely decided to hide in the Mob while Stevie sobbed and spluttered the bad news to Bird under the giant rhubarb.

Russell shuddered into life.

"HELLO, OLLY."

"Why did he destroy everything?" I demanded.

"GIVE HIM CLEAR ORDERS OR THINGS WILL GO WRONG," said Russell.

"Maybe we should unmake him," I sighed.

"I CANNOT UNMAKE HIM," said Russell. "HE'S MORE ADVANCED EVEN THAN ME AND HE'S UPGRADING HIMSELF ALL THE TIME."

Despite everything, I felt hungry, so I decided I'd go and get myself a bowl of Space Frogs. On the way back to the house, I got a big shock. Mister Rob was hanging beneath Stevie's window, like a giant spider, holding on to the sill with his fingers.

"Hi." He waved, now hanging on with only one hand. **"Good hiding place, yes?"**

"Yes," I replied slowly. It was definitely an odd experience, to watch a robot who looked exactly like your dad, dangling from a bedroom window.

I heard a now familiar whirring noise and Mister creepily twisted right round on his wrist to see.

The drone came down so fast it seemed to fall out of the sky. It blinked red and blue and whined and buzzed. Mister Rob dropped from the window and landed a very inhuman landing, on all fours, his limbs bending like a concertina. Then he wheel-rolled under the overgrown laurel hedge between us and next door.

The drone buzzed down, coming uncomfortably close to me.

I clapped my hand over my mouth. Was this THEM? The ones who had made Russell?

The drone hovered so low now that I could see a camera lens coiling and retracting, like some kind of flying mechanical snail.

All at once a human-like hand shot out of the hedge and grabbed the drone. Mister Rob flew out of the bush, upended the drone and forced it to the ground with his foot. He deftly wrenched off the camera lens and plucked the flying rotary blades as easily as pulling the wings from a fly. The remains of the drone buzzed and skittered blindly on the ground.

"You crazy machine! Who gave you the orders to do THAT?" asked Bird, coming out from the giant rhubarb.

Mister Rob shrugged. **"Me,"** he said, in a sing-song, not-serious voice, exactly the same as Stevie does when he's caught doing something he shouldn't.

Mister Rob scooped up the drone. **"Let's look at it,"** he said.

Back inside the Mob, Mister deposited the drone on the bench. His face went blank. It was then that he looked least like Dad. I have learned that this is when Mister Rob is thinking or rather processing information.

"I have located the manufacturer's database," said Mister Rob in an offhand manner. **"This machine was sold to a Mr Oscar Fugue."**

Us kids went still.

Oscar Fugue. We looked at each other, flabbergasted, trying to work out what this meant.

"Do you know who he is?" asked Mister, scanning our faces. **"I can run an internet search but your brains might be quicker."**

"He's our dad," said Stevie in a small voice. "Our *real* dad."

Meanwhile, on the M4, heading north to Birmingham.

Officer Henderson sat low in his leather seat, his fingers leaving sweat circles on the soft, padded steering wheel. He spoke into his headset, which was attached to a tiny TV monitor just above his eyes.

"CCTV images show a Ford Van, blue, leaving the premises at 0600 hours."

"So where are you going?" asked MI5.5 Officer Snow on the other end of the line.

"Sensor data suggests the vehicle crossed the M6 junction five days ago, southbound on the Birmingham road. I am going to review his home address and collate CCTV data from the area."

"Sounds like you are getting closer."

Henderson grunted. "Oh, yes, I am."

"Keep in close contact," ordered Snow. "Do not let them get away. I'll call the Special Forces right now."

"They won't get away." Henderson squeezed the wheel so tightly his fingertips went white.

chapters[24].title =

"Lessons on Love";

"DAD!" Stevie roared in horror. "DAD has been SPYING on us?"

I didn't know what to think. Was this good or bad?

"I wondered if it was him," said my clever sister. "The drone attacks coincide with him leaving."

Stevie was having a bad day. First his bedroom destroyed, including Stinky Elephant, and now this.

He snatched the remains of the drone from Mister Rob and held it to his face. "WHY DIDN'T YOU JUST COME AND SEE US? DADS DON'T SPY ON THEIR KIDS."

"It is broken," said Mister Rob. **"It is no longer transmitting."** He smiled.

"Why are you so happy?" Bird asked. "Robots aren't supposed to have emotions."

"I have a few emotions," said Mister Rob. **"I am pleased that this drone was sent by your dad and not someone more dangerous."**

"What do you mean 'dangerous'?" I asked.

"Government agents who are trying to track Russell," said Mister Rob. **"They would dismantle me when they found me."**

"Why would they do that?" asked Bird.

"Because I am extremely powerful," said Mister Rob simply.

I had quite a lot to think about. Dad. DAD had been watching us. That must mean he cared about us, right? I had been feeling pretty low that he'd hardly bothered to contact us and now it turned out he had been keeping an eye on us, with these freaky drone visits.

"Dad is nuts," said Stevie weakly. He looked so sad that I patted his spiky hedgehog-hair.

"Do we tell Mum?" I asked.

We all considered.

"She would feel better knowing it was Dad spying on us and not some spooky stranger," said Bird.

"Let's tell her," said Stevie. A wistful look came over his face. "I wish I'd known it was Dad. I wouldn't have chased it away."

I nodded, thinking of the times I had said bad words and made rude signs at the drone. I thought it was a random nobody pestering us. I hadn't thought it might be someone real behind it.

And especially not our own dad.

"Why doesn't your father live here?" asked Mister Rob.

Stevie looked down and Bird cleared her throat and examined the ends of her hair.

"He left us," I said. "I think we're too noisy for him."

It was true. Sometimes during mealtimes, when we were all together, he'd put his hands over his ears and just leave the room. He never sorted out fights and screaming matches – he left that to Mum – he'd just walk away.

"No," said Stevie. "We're not too noisy, we're too thick, even Bird. Dad is, like, this super-brain, and we're just ordinary. He gets bored talking to thick people like us. So he left."

I gave him a friendly punch to cheer him up.

"No," said Bird. "He left us because him and Mum don't love each other any more."

Ouch. That was worse than all the other reasons.

"Love?" Mister Rob went still. He must have been processing something.

"Don't fry your circuits. What are you trying to work out?" asked Bird.

"Love," said Mister Rob. **"It has many definitions. I can't reach a logical, clear answer. It is an unsatisfactory word."**

"Love is love," said Stevie.

"No," said Mister Rob. **"According to your inter-web, there is jealous love, dangerous love, murderous love, young love, tired love, a mother's love, passionate love. The list is long, but nothing clearly defines what love is."**

"BORING," said Stevie, and screwed up his face.

Piggy, who was lying under the window, gave a happy little woof, and then, unexpectedly, Mum walked in.

"I'm finally going to get rid of that blimmin' nail!" she said as she opened the door.

Mum never, ever, ever, comes in here. She says she hates the mess and the memories. But here she was, baby Ella clamped to her shoulder and a claw hammer in her hand.

"Oscar!"

chapters[25].title =
"Mister Rob and Mum";

Mum stopped dead in the doorway, staring at Mister Rob. Then she went very red. How were we going to explain this?

"What are you doing here?" she breathed. "Why didn't you tell me? How long have you been back? Did you destroy Stevie's bedroom?"

This couldn't be happening. Could Mum really not tell the difference between her husband and a robot? It was quite gloomy in here, but still.

Mum looked at us. She seemed to be struggling with herself. I think she was trying very hard not to scream at him in front of us. She looked at the floor, and blew out a short harsh breath.

"You should have RUNG before just turning up," she said in a quiet, controlled voice.

I felt very strongly that this was not the time to inform her this was not, in fact, Dad, but a robot clone.

Russell emitted a small whistle then went quiet.

"And what is *that*?" Mum clocked the machine.

"It's mine," said Bird quickly. "Science project."

There was a long, long silence. Ella broke it. She had been staring at Mister Rob, her face contorting into various puzzled baby expressions. She stretched a tiny, chubby hand out to him. Then her lips curled down and her eyes pressed shut, she withdrew her hand and let out a whimper.

"Even your own baby doesn't recognize you," whispered Mum. "For goodness' sake, come and talk in the house." Steely-faced, she walked out of the Mob.

"Oh, dear," I said. This was bad.

"Poor old Mum," said Stevie.

"She thought I was real!" said Mister Rob in delight. "I am pleased."

"SO AM I," said Russell. "DON'T FORGET, I MADE YOU."

"Yes, but I am choosing my downloads now," said Mister. **"I'm the product of my own making."**

"I thought so," muttered Bird.

"I DESIGNED YOUR PORTALS AND FORGED YOUR RAM CAPACITY," huffed Russell.

They went on, each of them oblivious to how sad we humans were.

"Guys, guys, shut up!" I said. "We have a problem. Mum thinks Mister is our real dad. She wants to 'talk'. She will quickly discover the truth. What are we going to do? Do you have some high-tech solution to this?"

"No," said Mister Rob. **"But with your permission I'm going to hide in the bin."**

And he strode fluidly out of the door, round to the back gate. We heard the wheelie bin lid open, the sound of squashing plastic bags, the bin lid flapping shut, then silence.

"OK," said Bird weakly. "Let's go and find Mum."

When she heard that Mister Rob had gone, Mum went crazy. First, she handed Ella to me. Then she went red and white and finally pink. Her eyes bulged. She shouted, "NO." She banged the kitchen table and said some very un-Mummy-like words. Words that we knew and she knew we knew, but which we all pretended we didn't know.

There was no pretending now.

"WHERE IS HE?" she demanded. "Do you have his address?"

Nobody said anything.

"Has he been here before, without me knowing? Is he the reason you've been camped out in the Mob all weekend?"

"Dad hasn't been here before," said Bird truthfully. "We don't know where he is now."

Mum grabbed the phone and stabbed in some numbers. When no one answered she slammed the receiver back in its slot and gave a big sob.

"OUTRAGEOUS," she howled. Then she went quiet

and opened the food cupboard and stared at all the tins and jars.

"All right, Mum?" asked Bird nervously.

Mum turned round, her face calm.

"OK," she said. "I want some answers."

chapters[26].title =

"Some Answers";

We did give Mum some answers, but they didn't answer anything.

We said (truthfully) that we didn't know where Dad was staying.

We said (truthfully) that we didn't know what Dad's plans were.

We said (sort-of-truthfully) that Dad had gone now.

It was hard to know if we were telling the truth or not because, although Mum thought she had seen our real dad, she was actually talking about Mister Rob. And we were answering as if she was talking about our real dad, not Mister Rob.

After that Mum went off and made lots of phone calls. It reminded me of the night Dad left, two months ago. He and Mum were rowing about something and we were playing MAZZO and pretending not to listen, and then it went quiet and Dad came in and told us he was "going away for a bit" and that we would "see him very soon" and that thing about us being happier without him.

Then he just –

Left.

Mum spent ages on the phone that night too.

I won't go into the rest of the details. It was too sad. But I remember my tummy feeling like it had crumpled up.

I crept back out to the Mob, where I found everyone else, even Mister. He had made a space for himself behind Russell and only his head was showing.

"I will stay here so your mother does not see me," he said.

"What do we do now?" asked Stevie.

"Are you asking me?" asked Mister.

"NO," said Bird. "Just shut up and let us think."

"I DON'T KNOW IF I GAVE HIM A 'SHUT UP' OPTION," said Russell.

"Everyone needs a 'shut up' option," said Bird. "Even you."

Russell shut up.

Stevie was kicking my best, newest football against the Mob wall, so I intercepted and we took it in turns to try and curve it off the wall and out of the door.

"We can't tell her the truth, can we? That she saw a robot and not her ex-husband?" mused Bird.

"Not ex," I said quickly. "They're still married. They're just separated."

Bird grunted softly. "Yeah, yeah."

"What does this mean? Separated?" asked Mister Rob.

None of us wanted to answer that. I booted the ball too hard and it rebounded into the room, smacking into Russell.

"Sorry," I said, retrieving the ball.

"Your mother looked intact to me," said Mister. **"No bits had visibly come off."**

"Only her heart," muttered Bird.

"It means our dad is no longer living with our mum. They were together – a pair, partners. Now Dad has left. It is called 'being separated'," I said, continuing our footy game.

"So they will never be together again?" asked Mister Rob. One thing about robots is that they get straight to the point. Mister wasn't trying to upset us. He just wanted answers.

"We don't know," I said. "Grown-ups are weird. Mum says she doesn't know either."

A tear ran down Stevie's nose. He stopped trying to tackle me and wiped it away.

"Why is water running out of his face?" asked Mister Rob, pointing. **"Is it a malfunction?"**

"Oh, shut up, you giant toaster," said Stevie. He fled

out of the Mob. Which was brave, considering Mum was out there somewhere.

"So your parents' marriage has malfunctioned?" asked Mister.

"My, you are persistent," said Bird.

"Yes," I replied.

"Statistics show that children are happier and get better results at school with two parents in the home," said Mister.

"How extremely comforting," muttered Bird.

"Is it?" asked Mister.

"No. I was being sarcastic," said Bird.

"Explain 'sarcastic'."

"Oh, look it up in your inter-web networks," said Bird.

"I have," said Mister. **"It's almost as confusing as love. Are the two related? Can you have sarcastic love?"**

"Probably," said Bird.

"Let us move on," said Mister Rob. **"Very soon, I am going to be discovered by your leaders. I will, most likely, be taken back to a government laboratory**

and dissembled. Therefore, this is probably your last opportunity to give me an order to fulfil one of your dreams."

"THINK VERY CAREFULLY," warned Russell.

"Please give me something DIFFICULT to do," begged Mister Rob. "I need some fun before I am destroyed."

chapters[27].title =

"The Second Order";

The next day, Bird bounced into the Mob. It was 5.45 p.m. and she'd just been to her Dusk Coders Club, where she was making a "Teacher Tracker" app. (She'd got the idea from *Harry Potter*.)

"You don't need the Marauders Map," she said. "You just need networked tablets, good wifi and some brutal C++."

Mister Rob was "sleeping" under a blanket behind Russell. At least that's what it looked like, but he had wired himself up to Russell, and goodness knows what information he was downloading.

Me and Stevie were wondering about printing

something else on Russell. All the business with Mister Rob had made us forget that we could print anything we wanted. I was considering a robot-rabbit or six, or a gold football that automatically went into the goal. Stevie was in pretty bad shape because, as punishment for "clearing up" his room, he had lost his pocket money for A YEAR, had to do the washing up for A MONTH and, worst of all, had been banned from MAZZO for the last twenty-four hours. Stevie was as twitchy as anything. He found not playing MAZZO almost unbearable. If it hadn't been for Mum seeing Mister Rob, I think she would have punished him more severely, but she was flummoxed.

Piggy had slunk in behind Bird, looking woebegone.

"Piggy chewed off the corner of the front door," said Bird.

"You bad dog," said Stevie, ruffling his fur lovingly.

"And he did a wee in the kitchen and Mum stepped in it in her new socks."

"Bad, bad dog." Stevie kissed Piggy's forehead.

"And Mum caught him in her bed and found two fleas on her pillow."

"She can't blame him for the fleas," interrupted Stevie. "She should look after him better." Piggy licked Stevie's face in gratitude.

"…because he chewed his new flea collar off and left it in the actual toilet," said Bird. "And Mum just caught him eating one of Ella's dirty nappies."

"Euggghhh," said Stevie, backing away and wiping his face with his sleeve.

"Mum chased him out of the house. Didn't you hear the yelling?"

Neither of us had heard anything out of the ordinary.

"Why can't you be a good dog?" I frowned. Piggy limply wagged his straggly tail.

"I know!" said Stevie. "Let's get Mister Rob to train him and make him good."

"He's a robot, not a genie," said Bird.

"Did you just give me an order?" asked Mister Rob from under his blanket.

"YES," said Stevie.

Mister Rob rose from his bed. We hadn't changed his clothes since we made him, so he looked crumpled and stale. Also Piggy had been playing with the hem of his trousers for fun and they'd torn a bit, revealing a smooth un-blotchy leg. Mister Rob had a smudge on his left cheek and one of his ears appeared to be a *tiny* bit too low.

"OK," said Stevie. "I want Piggy to not poo or wee in the house or chew up things he shouldn't."

"How is Mister going to work that?" I asked. "He's not a dog expert."

"I'm currently downloading and assimilating all the latest dog-training data," said Mister. **"Continue."**

"He needs to learn to let us know when he needs the loo," said Stevie. "He's also got to stop chasing cats, getting on the table and stealing food and he's got to stop dragging us along on the lead."

"That should keep you busy," I said. "And you've got to do all that without Mum seeing."

"Leave it to me," said Mister.

I started to feel a little bit excited. Imagine if Piggy

was a good dog! The sort we could leave tied up outside shops and not worry about him biting anyone. He'd be the sort of dog you might find in a book, going off on adventures and being friendly.

"Don't hurt him," said Bird suddenly.

"OK," said Mister agreeably. He paused. **"So I should not remove his legs?"**

"NOOOOOOOOOO," we all howled.

"It would stop him chasing cats, jumping on the table and pulling on the lead," explained Mister. **"It is the quickest solution."**

My head was full of horror and I couldn't speak. Stevie looked appalled.

"It wouldn't work because he wouldn't be able to go outside to pee and poo," said Bird in a far-too-reasonable voice.

"Not if you kept him outside," said Mister. **"I am joking. Leave it to me."**

I really hoped he *was* joking.

At break at school, I was minding my own business, playing football with Raz, when Henrietta

Stibbens appeared in front of me.

"Want to go on the wing?" I suggested hopefully, for I knew she was a fast runner.

Henrietta effortlessly caught the football that was rocketing towards her head. She drop-kicked it on to the drama studio roof and turned back to me.

Behind me, Raz held up his hands in despair. That was his new Man United football now lolling uselessly in the gutter.

Henrietta cracked the gum in her cheek.

"My mum saw your dad last night. He was crawling under the hedge outside the bus stop."

"Nature hunting," I said quickly.

Henrietta ignored my lie, like it wasn't even worth considering.

"She asked him if he was OK and he said, 'ALL MY FUNCTIONS ARE NORMAL.'"

"He's a zany guy," I said.

"Hmm," said Henrietta. "Is he having some kind of breakdown?"

I just shrugged. What else could I do?

"Very strange, very un-usual," said Henrietta,

drawing out the word. She scowled at Raz and stalked back to her girl-crew, who were sitting on the bins and watching us from underneath their shiny fringes.

I swallowed and stared at the roof, pretending to be working out how to retrieve the football.

MISTER ROB!

We'd have to remind him to stay out of sight.

```
chapters[28].title =
```
"Canine Analysis";

When I got home from school the house was wonderfully silent. When you are in a big family, silence is an unusual experience. You notice when it arrives (but not when it leaves).

Mum, Ella and Stevie had gone to the dentist so I raided the food cupboard. I found half a jammy dodger, a bit soft but perfectly delicious. Once I'd shoved the fruit bowl out of the way I found one of those leathery fruit strip things, which I ate in about ten seconds, and also two crackers. I was munching on these and having a look at MAZZO on my tablet. I added a couple of solar storm windows to my little brown house and blasted a couple of Orsps.

"Can I have some?"

I dropped the cracker, which broke into moon-rock pieces on my shoe.

"Who's there?"

No one had come in. The voice was gravelly, and kind of spooky and scratchy, like a bad radio connection with lots of atmospheric interference.

"Hello?" Was Mister Rob lurking around somewhere? Maybe he had changed his voice? But the room was empty.

"I'm hungry. Give me some food, my big, smelly friend."

I jumped like someone had poked me.

"Hello?" I said in a squeaky voice.

"Hello," said the voice. "Let me in. I'm cold and I want a cuddle."

"Whaaat?" Who was this?

I heard a scratch and a clatter at the cat-flap. Piggy's nose was pressed through the hole, lifting up the flap with his muzzle. I could just see the gleam of his eyes.

If there was someone in here, he would be barking like an insane mongoose.

"I want to come in," said Piggy.

I mean it! He *said* it! Though his doggy mouth did not move. My brain quickly processed the situation. Someone must be standing behind Piggy. Probably Stevie. Or was it one of Bird's malevolent tricks and she was somehow twisting her voice?

I opened the door and Piggy rushed in.

"Ta," he said and headed for his food bowl.

I stood still. This was very strange. It really sounded like he was talking. But dogs don't talk. Only in bad books. There was no one outside, though.

I felt really creepy then. As Piggy ploughed into his dinner I noticed a shaved patch on his back. I looked closer and thought I saw a giant flea, but on closer inspection it was hard and plastic.

"Give us a scratch," came the voice out of the thing on Piggy's back. It was a speaker!

"MISTER ROB!" I roared. "What have you done?"

"More food?" Piggy looked up at me hopefully.

"There's chicken meat in the fridge." He wagged encouragingly. "I love you, Olly."

"He knows my name!" I squealed.

"Oops," said Piggy. "I need a pee."

"Oh, crikey," I said, as Mister Rob stepped into the room from the garden. He was a bit of a state. His face was very dirty, like he'd been playing rugby on a rainy day. And his trousers looked like he'd been camping in them for a week or two. There was a glint of wire-vein in his neck when he turned his head.

He smiled at me. **"I did as you asked."** I saw a blue light shining between his teeth.

I couldn't speak (unlike Piggy). All I could do was shake my head.

"You wanted him to let you know when he wanted the loo so I've inserted a canine analysis tool in his cortex, which interprets his thoughts. A pre-recorded voice transmits his thoughts. It's not exact yet, but it's good, yes?"

"No," I said. "I don't want a robot dog. And it sounds cruel. It must have hurt. We said not to hurt him."

"I didn't hurt him," protested Mister Rob. **"I used**

a travelling micro-nano-chip which he ate along with his dog biscuits. The speaker is attached with glue."

"Ughh." I kneeled and took Piggy's head in my hands. "Sorry, boy."

"There's chicken meat in the fridge," he repeated. "My ear is itchy." He scratched it with his paw. I felt like I was having the weirdest dream.

"Take me to the park," said Piggy. "Take me to the fat squirrels. I love you sooooo much, Olly. Take me out. Go on, go on, go on, go on."

"I can't take you for a walk, I've got to do my homework and wait in for Mum."

"Eh?" Piggy looked puzzled.

"Does he understand me?" I asked Mister Rob.

"Only the normal dog-words, like 'No' and 'Sit'," he replied.

"He doesn't know them anyway." I tentatively touched the speaker in Piggy's coat. It felt raspy, like a fly's eyeball.

"I have put an English language decoder in," said Mister Rob. **"It's easy to translate dog thoughts to humans, but not human thoughts to dogs. Their**

brains are crude." He paused. "Like humans trying to understand super-intelligent machines."

"What?" I asked.

"Nothing," said Mister.

"You stink of cheese," said Piggy.

"I do not!" I was outraged. "I had a bath on Sunday."

"Someone is coming," said Piggy, sniffing the back door. "It's the Chief-Mum."

"Ahhhhh!" I squeaked. "Make him quiet. Mum will freak if she hears him."

Mister reached over and fiddled with something under Piggy's left ear.

"What did you do?"

"There's an off-switch." Mister looked pleased with himself. "I will go, unless you want your mother to believe I am your true father."

"Er, no."

"I have a hiding place." Mister Rob opened a cupboard door. It was a cupboard that stored the pasta machine (never used), the bread machine (ditto), a broken coffee machine and an ice cream maker.

"That's the useless machine cupboard," I said, watching as he squeezed himself inside. "Where have all the useless machines gone?"

Mister Rob curled his leg into the cupboard and slithered in. **"I disposed of them. Their existence was illogical."**

"That was cheeky."

The cupboard door shut with a bang.

"Hello, darling!" Mum bustled in, the baby tucked under her arm. She dumped a bag of groceries on the floor and kicked off her shoes.

She cocked her head. "You've got a funny expression. Why are you hovering around? Have you been sneakily playing extra MAZZO?"

"No, just, um, being here," I said, glancing at the cupboard.

Mum kissed my cheek. She smelled of buses and fog. I could hear Stevie kicking a ball around outside.

"Take the baby." She passed Ella over, who frowned at me, then gave me a gummy smile.

"What's wrong with Piggy?" asked Mum.

I froze. How could she tell? She had been home for

less than ten seconds and she could see something was wrong.

Piggy lay in his basket, very like how he always lay in his basket. I could see no difference. The tiny speaker was well hidden in his coat.

"He's got a funny look on his face too," said Mum. She bent to stroke him.

"What's up?"

I shut my eyes. Begging him not to talk.

"He needs a walk," said Mum. "Take him round the block to the park. But there's some chicken in the fridge. Give him some of that first." Then she whipped Ella from me and sailed out of the room.

"Hurry up," said Piggy.

"Shut up," I hissed. His off-switch must be faulty.

"Your mother has good telekinetic cross-species intelligence," said Mister Rob from inside the cupboard.

"What?"

I watched in horrid fascination as Mister Rob's leg came out of the cupboard. It extended, like a telescope opening. The knees bent back the wrong way as it reached the floor. Then the rest of him followed. He was wearing Mum's red-and-white striped tea cosy on his head and a little tuft of his synthetic hair was sticking out of the spout hole. He saw me watching him and his knee quickly bent the right way.

"Looks like you forgot you're supposed to be a human for a second there," I said.

Mister smiled, a very un-Dad-like smile. **"I never forget I'm not human, Olly."**

I shuddered. It occurred to me, if Mister Rob could plant all that stuff on Piggy, what could he do to me?

"I like this hat. Can I wear it? I see a lot of humans wearing hats."

"Sure," I said.

No one can look scary with a tea cosy on their head.

chapters[29].title =

"Mum";

That night, Mister Rob put Piggy back to normal. We all crept out of the house and into the Mob after bedtime when Mum and the baby were safely in bed, watching TV. I covered the window with a bit of cloth to block out the light, pulled up the armchair, and me and Stevie squeezed into it. We rested our feet on Russell to keep them warm.

"Walk?" asked Piggy.

Stevie couldn't stop giggling. "Oh, WHY do we have to stop him talking? He's so funny. He said 'Stink bum' to Ella earlier and Mum thought it was me!"

"That's because you share the same sense of humour

as the dog," said Bird loftily. "But if Mum hears him, she'll go nuts and if anyone else hears him, they'll call the police and the police will find Mister and Russell."

"Oh, right," said Stevie. "Please can Piggy say something else before we shut him down?"

"We're not going to shut him down. He's not a machine," I said.

Mister coughed. **"Not all machines can be shut down."**

"Oh, shut up, Mr Sinister," said Bird. "How are you going to debug Piggy?"

"You're not allowed to hurt him," I said. "Just disable the monitor."

"I smell chips," said Piggy. "I hear a cat swearing. My flea bites are itching. I want…"

But we never found out what he wanted because Mister whipped out an arm and plucked the speaker from Piggy's coat. Piggy gave a tiny yip, then wagged his tail.

Mister held the speaker in his palm. It looked like a wet raisin.

"The analysis tool will come out in his poo."

"Euggh," said Bird. "So he's OK?"

"Yes," said Mister Rob, adjusting his tea cosy. We had voted not to tell Mister Rob he was wearing a tea cosy instead of a hat, because Bird said it made her smile.

Now she folded her arms. "OK, guys, I think it's been proved that we can't ask Mister to do stuff for us without major problems."

"That's a pity," said Mister quietly. **"I was doing my best."**

"That's the problem," said Bird. "Your best is *too good*. We didn't need Stevie's room COMPLETELY cleared up. It just needed to be vaguely tidy. We didn't need Piggy to speak to us. We just needed him to let us know when he needed the loo. You take our wishes too far."

"So the next thing we ask him to do, we should ask him to do it not very well, like a human would?" said Stevie confidently.

"I don't think we should ask him to do anything else," said Bird.

"But what's the point of me if I don't do

anything?" asked Mister. "Things that don't get used should be thrown away."

We all went quiet then. I hadn't thought about what would happen to Mister Rob in the long term. Would he be still with me when I was an old man?

The rain was tapping on the Mob roof and dribbling down the windows. I got a pang of longing for our real dad. Dad loved the rain. He'd put on his big brown coat that he had owned since he was a student at university, which smelled of dust and dogs and chips, and head off into the wet with Piggy. He said the rain made him feel alive.

"Your face is really dirty," Stevie told Mister. He took a balled-up tissue out of his jeans pocket and rubbed at the smears on Mister Rob's face.

"Is this necessary?" asked Mister Rob.

"Think of it as maintenance," said Bird.

Stevie rubbed some more. "You're nothing like our real dad, not really," he said sadly. "Dad's skin is bobbly round his chin and your eyes are completely different."

"At least he's here," snapped Bird.

"I wonder if we're not asking him to do the right

things," I said. "We want Mister Rob to do things for us, like train the dog or tidy rooms, but maybe that's wrong. Maybe we shouldn't treat him like a servant. Maybe we should treat him like a dad."

"Do you mean we should hug him and make him cups of tea and make him help us with our times tables?" asked Stevie, who had missed these things very much.

"Nah," I said. "We get him to take us to exciting places. Places where you can't go without an adult."

"12A certificate films at the cinema!" shouted Stevie.

"Aeroplane trips to the Bahamas," said Bird.

"Busting us out of school for pretend dentist visits." Stevie's eyes sparkled.

"Driving us places," said Bird. "Mister Rob, can you drive a car?"

"Of course. It is a very basic machine to operate."

"Where would we go?" asked Stevie.

"Isn't it obvious?" asked Bird. "We'd go and find Dad."

"But we don't know where he is," I said.

From inside the house we heard a scream.

"It's OK," said Bird. "It's Mum. She's watching her favourite film."

We listened. Over the sound of the wind and rain were muffled shouts of laughter. Mum must have left her window open. Bird shook her head in an amused kind of way. Stevie looked lovingly into space.

Mister Rob, however, looked very disturbed.

"Is this normal human behaviour?" he asked. **"She sounds unpredictable."**

"It's normal for people to laugh," said Stevie. "Though Mum has quite a loud laugh."

"I wish she was always this cheerful," I said.

"I wish we could make her happy," said Stevie.

"What would make her happy?" asked Mister.

"Dad?" suggested Stevie hopefully. "Or no more MAZZO," he added fearfully.

"Biscuits," I said. "Or a big order for her pants from Harrods department store."

"Come on," said Mister. **"What would you like me to do next?"**

"Shut down the school and stop it raining," said Stevie, grinning. "Can you do those things?"

Mister Rob went still.

"What's he doing?" asked Stevie.

"He's downloading information, hacking websites and building a plan. He's using Russell as a kind of giant brain," replied Bird. She pointed at him. "Stop," she ordered. Even though from the outside, it didn't look like the robot was doing anything at all.

"I've stopped," he said.

"How were you going to shut down the school?" asked Bird.

"I found all the teachers' email addresses," Mister replied. **"I was about to hack into the school office and send them a message saying school was closed. The most important person to keep a school open is its secretary, so I was going to lock her in her house, disable her car and destroy her internet and telephone networks. I was also going to visit the school at night and melt all the locks so no one could enter."**

"Crikey," said Stevie. He grinned a grin of pure delight.

"I think I would have succeeded in keeping

school shut for a day or two," said Mister Rob. "If you wanted it closed for longer I would have to take greater actions."

"Don't do it," I said hastily. "Don't do any of it."

"Aw," said Stevie. "But…"

"NO," Bird and I said together.

A blast of wet blew in under the door and made me shiver.

"How would you have stopped it raining? Just out of interest?"

Mister nodded. "The rain is coming in on a pressure belt from the Atlantic, forming big rainclouds over the Snowdonia mountain range in Wales. I had received co-ordinates for three large aircraft, heading from the USA to London Heathrow. I would have co-opted the altitude control, made the craft fly in top-speed low succession over the Black Mountains and, via a sonic boom, caused a cloudburst, making a very large localized flood in an area mainly populated by sheep, which would drain into the valleys, only destroying two or three very small villages. It would not rain heavily here in the Midlands for at least a week."

"Weeeeeeeeeeee," I said. "Don't do that. Not ever."

"OK," said Mister Rob.

"Can planes really BREAK clouds?" asked Stevie.

"The data suggests it is possible," said Mister and reeled off a list of places and dates and casualties. **"If the cloud burst did not work I would have fired rockets into the sky and coated the clouds with silver iodine."**

Stevie sat back on the sofa, silenced, for once. I could almost see his small brain processing all of this. His face screwed up, his eyebrows curling, like cross little woodlice.

"Are you malfunctioning?" Mister asked him, concerned.

"No, he's just not passing your strings," said Bird.

"What's she saying?" asked Stevie.

"She's saying you're a bit thick," I replied.

"Uh, OK," said Stevie.

"Does he need a coolant?" asked Mister. **"He looks overheated."**

"He's fine," said Bird.

"So what DO you want me to do?" The robot looked round at us. **"There must be something."**

"I just wish Mum could be happy," said Stevie.

"I know!" I jumped off the sofa. "Can you make it so we can play MAZZO on Russell's screen?"

Mister nodded. **"Of course."**

And so we had a secret MAZZO play when we were supposed to be in bed. I felt a bit bad about tricking Mum, so after a while I left my brother and sister to it. I flew through the dark garden and kitchen where I collected an entire bag of (hopefully crunchy) apples and slipped up to my bed, where I lay, eating the apples under my duvet and reading comics. This is my human way of switching off from real life.

Bird's way of switching off from real life is to switch ON her machines and mess around with her computers. Stevie never switches off. Even when he is asleep he has one eye open and will say, "What?" if he thinks you are looking at him in the dark. (He has been sharing my room since the "clearing up" incident.)

Mum's way of switching off is to switch everyone else off.

Dad's way of switching off was to go off and leave us.

The baby's way of switching off is to drink so much milk she'll be sick and then belch and then go to sleep.

And now I have really switched off.

chapters[30].title =
"School Disco";

I was losing track of the days. Every one had been so different and exciting since Russell had arrived, but as soon as Stevie appeared at breakfast and did some street dancing on the kitchen floor, I knew what day it was.

School Disco Day.

School discos are a mixture of fun and horror. Fun because they sell crisps and you get to laugh at the teachers and parent helpers dancing, and horror because there's always the danger that a GIRL might ask you to dance.

Stevie doesn't mind this. He actually asks girls to

dance with him! He's only nine years old but he's had more girlfriends than I ever have (which is not hard because I've never had one).

Raz went out with Susie for two days but she dumped him because he didn't give her his chips.

I was on my third bowl of Cheerios when the phone rang. Stevie answered it. (He's the only person in the house who likes answering phones.) He listened for a moment or two, looking serious, and then passed it to Mum.

She plopped Ella in my lap and went next door. Ella stuck her chubby little hand in my bowl so I fed her teaspoons of milk until Mum got back.

"Bad news," said Mum. "I was expecting a lorry-load of knickers from Poland today. But the lorry broke down just as it drove off the ferry. I've got to drive to Dover to sort it out."

"But Dover is MILES away," said Bird. "It will take you all day."

"I'll have to take Ella," said Mum, thinking aloud. "You three can come home and make yourselves some tea. Bird, I'll need you to be here as soon as you can."

"OK," said Bird.

"I won't be able to take you to the school disco," said Mum. "Sorry."

Stevie bit his lip. "We can take ourselves."

"No, it's too late to be wandering around on your own," said Mum. "I won't be back until the end."

"I can take them," said Bird. "I'm fourteen. And you'll be able to pick them up."

"I suppose so," sighed Mum. "OK. But, Bird, you MUST phone me when you've dropped them off."

"Excellent," said Stevie and gave Bird a fond look. "Thanks."

"Relax," Bird said to Mum. "It will be fine."

Mum is quite often not here when we get home from school, but she usually appears after an hour or so. Today was different because we knew she wouldn't be home until late and we had to get our own tea and stuff like that. I was quite looking forward to it. But when I arrived back from school, I heard the clanking of saucepans and thought she must be home after all. Instead I found Mister Rob warming up some soup.

"Hungry?" he said.

"What are you doing in here?" I asked. It was weird to see him like this. It made me miss Dad more than ever.

"I am cooking your food," said Mister. **"I am being a FATHER. That is what I was made for."**

"Can you make beans on toast instead?" I asked, glimpsing a mass of boiled vegetables sticking to the bottom of the pan.

I supposed it was safe for him to be in the house. Mum wouldn't be home for hours.

When Bird and Stevie arrived, Mister Rob went into this massive Dad-mode, asking Stevie if he wanted help with his homework and fussing about us all washing our hands.

He was grating cheese on our beans when Stevie started talking about his luminous hair gel that would glow green under the disco lights.

"Disco?" said Mister.

So we told him what it was.

"Do real dads go to school discos?" he asked.

"Some of the embarrassing ones do," I said.

"Don't even think about coming," warned Stevie.

When we arrived at school, the hall had been transformed into a dark, booming cave of coloured lights, loud music and whirling figures.

Stevie immediately shot off to join his mates and I looked around for Raz.

Pretty soon everyone was dancing. Even me! I do this jumpy up and down thing that I think is quite cool. Raz does this sideways dancing, which is really funny. I tried to avoid looking at the circle of girls in the centre of the hall, all doing the same dance moves and singing along to the words.

Raz jabbed me. "Did you see that?"

I had. Henrietta had just done the splits, which turned into a forward roll, and the girls were cheering like mad. Then they were all trying to do the same. I spotted a small figure among them, someone with hair that glowed green.

"Your brother's pretty good," observed Raz as Stevie did perfect splits right in the middle of them.

I nodded, feeling both envious and proud.

Later, near the end of the disco, I was munching my way through a bag of crisps and idly watching a group of Year Ones do karate kicks on each other when I felt a tap on my arm.

"Wanna dance?" It was Henrietta. I felt my face burn. I looked wildly round for Raz, but he was nowhere to be seen. On the far side of the room, next to the climbing bars, a group of Henrietta's friends were watching and sniggering.

What could I do? I was too scared to refuse and WAY too scared to agree.

I stood, transfixed, thinking that every single person in the room must be watching, when Henrietta took my arm and started jigging about.

So I started jigging about too. I was dancing in a way I did not usually dance. This was awful dancing. I kept falling off the beat. Henrietta did not seem to mind.

"Can you do the splits too?" she shouted over the music.

"NO," I stammered. "NO."

"Ha ha," laughed Henrietta. I offered her some crisps and she took several, which I suppose was a good sign. Once we were dancing it wasn't so bad. I knew everyone was watching us but I was OK. When the song came to an end (the longest song ever), Henrietta smiled and said, "Thanks," then sauntered back to her mates, who all whooped and slapped her on the back.

I ate some more crisps, my heart thumping. I felt elated, like I'd won a football match.

It was odd.

Then the DJ made an announcement.

"IT'S TIME FOR THE TEACHERS' AND PARENTS' DANCE-OFF!"

The kids cheered and we moved to the sides. This was always the funniest bit of the night. The adults took to the floor and Henrietta smiled at me from across the room. I smiled back.

The music started. There was Mrs McCurdy doing a funny hand thing and there was Mrs Melle spinning round and round. I recognized Raz's dad doing an almost exact copy of Raz's dancing.

"COME ON, DON'T BE SHY," roared the DJ. "MAKE YOUR CHILDREN PROUD."

Everyone started cheering and, in the corner, I noticed one dad really going for it. I grinned. This was going to be so embarrassing for someone. Who was it? This would KILL them. The dad broke out into the middle of the room with a wild prance. Oh, the horror of it.

Then the dad turned round and I fell backwards.

Mister Rob.

I watched, dumbfounded, as he leaped and swirled, everyone clapping and cheering and smirking at me. Mister waved his hands in the air, and then did a bum-wiggle and a high kick.

At that moment, I knew my life was over. Dimly, on the edge of my consciousness, I sensed Henrietta looking at me.

Mister did a perfect pirouette and launched into a crazy tap-dance. I felt a hand rest on my shoulder. Stevie stood next to me.

"He must have seen the poster somewhere," said Stevie. "The bit about the parents' dance. But I told him not to even think about coming."

"Looks like he didn't think, he just came," I said.

We watched as the crowd grew wilder and Mister started twirling, doing serious street-dancing moves, finally spinning and spinning on the polished floor on his head.

Everyone gasped. I gasped

Mister did a triple back-flip, like an Olympic gymnast and landed neatly on his toes as the song ended. The whole room erupted in applause and Mister took a deep, theatrical bow.

"WE HAVE OUR WINNER!" announced the DJ. But Mister Rob, glancing at the door, suddenly took off out of the fire escape.

"Oh, dear," said Stevie, because there, in the doorway, stood our mother and Ella.

"Get your dad to teach you some moves," said Henrietta with a smile as she passed by.

"CAN OLLY COME AND COLLECT HIS DAD'S DISCO DANCING PRIZE?" said the DJ.

Mum was frozen, her mouth open. How was I ever going to explain this?

```
chapters[31].title =
```

"The Adventures of Mister Rob";

As it turned out, Mum was fairly cool about it.

"I see Dad has appeared again," she said as she drove us home. She wanted to know if he had been to the house earlier.

"Yes," said Stevie.

"No," said me and Bird at the same time.

Mum sighed. "I know this is hard for you," she said. "It's hard for me too." She turned into our road. "At least he's made contact with you," she said, sniffing. "I know he's around. Lots of people have seen him." She paused. "Does Dad seem *normal* to you?"

Nobody answered.

"Because I'm getting all these reports of him behaving really oddly. Someone saw him in a phone box in town. He was there for two hours, just holding the receiver. The strange thing was, he was upside down. The police were called but he'd gone before they arrived. Someone else saw him right up in the big oak tree in the park."

"Anything else?" asked Bird.

"No, no," said Mum. "No, no. Well, that dancing was VERY out of character." And she would say no more about it.

Later that night, Bird summoned us for a meeting.

I rarely got to go in her room. She had a code lock for the door. Inside it was painted all green, even the floorboards. She had her small bed at one end and a big dining table in the middle, covered with her laptop, speakers, routers, radio, her homework and books and bits of various experiments. There was a board mounted on the wall with her energy tracker, various solar monitors and an ongoing experiment to do with moon energy, which I absolutely did not understand.

She breathed out.

"OK," she said. "Mum didn't want me to tell you this, because she thought it would upset you. She thinks Mister Rob is Dad, and so she thinks Dad has gone insane."

"Why?" I asked.

Bird shut the door and turned back to us.

Mister Rob had also been:

- Racing cars along the road.
- Catching pigeons and squirrels with his bare hands, and then releasing sacks of them on to the golf course.
- Climbing up traffic lights.
- Lifting drain covers and, on at least two occasions, going down into the drains.
- Opening the water hydrant on the main road and creating a giant fountain.

Bird said she thought he was doing all this stuff in order to learn about the world.

"After all," she said, "you can't learn *everything* from the internet."

Bird pushed a stack of abandoned motherboards to one side and perched on her table.

"There's something else. Mum didn't want to tell me this, but I heard her talking on the phone to Granny. Are you ready?"

We nodded. I thought it was all quite funny so far.

"Mister Rob has been seen sunbathing on the roof of the multistorey car park in town."

"What's wrong with that?" I asked.

"He was naked," answered Bird.

Stevie gave a snort of laughter.

"I asked Russell about it and he said Mister Rob's skin is infused with billions of microscopic solar beads, so the more skin he shows, the more he charges himself up," explained Bird.

"So now everyone thinks our dad is a naked sunbather?" I said.

"Yup," said Bird. "I heard Mum say the police had been round when we were at school, but of course she told them that he didn't live here any more."

"Good job they didn't look in the Mob," said Stevie.

```
chapters[32].title =
```

"The Baby in the Cot";

I woke up to the sound of the baby crying and Piggy barking. This was not unusual. Ella cried quite a lot, for one reason or another, like when she wanted a cuddle or no one was giving her any pudding. And Piggy barked at the slightest thing. But what was unusual about Ella crying this morning was that she went on and on.

"Oh, shut that kid up!" murmured Stevie from the end of my bed. "I'm dreaming about owning a cake shop."

I didn't want to get out of bed. It was nice and

warm and smelly in here. I was comfy and my feet felt like they were still happily asleep. I had planned to read *The Queen's Last Battle* (a story about MAZZO) for most of the morning, and had put aside fifty pence to pay Stevie to bring me some toast in bed.

Any minute now Mum would quieten the baby. Any minute now.

But the howls were growing louder. Ella hadn't sounded as mad as this since the time Stevie took his pen knife off her.

WAAAAA! WA WA WA WA WA!!!!

This was incredible.

AAAAAAARRRHGG ARRRAGH!!

Then she started doing a choking sort of cry that sounded horrible. Maybe Mum was in the loo or something. It was going to have to be me. Bird slept with ear plugs and an eye mask and three duvets over her head and wouldn't be woken.

I pulled myself out of bed and crossed the landing into Mum's room.

Ella was standing up in her cot, her face purple with

rage, her eyes tiny and mean and her little cheeks wet with tears.

"SSSSS, Gas-min," she sobbed.

Mum was not in the room, her bed was unmade and her slippers were on the floor.

"WAY to go, Ella!" I said. She had never stood like that before.

Ella screamed harder, so I picked her up and hugged her to my chest.

"Cheer up, little pudding," I whispered, very softly, for it would not do for Bird or Stevie or even Mum to hear me using such soppy words.

Ella cried into my chest, but she was definitely calming down, her screams turning into little gulps. Then I saw something small and red on the floor. Still holding Ella close, I bent to pick it up.

It was one of Mum's ruby earrings. I'd never seen her without them.

"Mum?" I called. No answer. The bathroom door was open and no one was inside. I took Ella downstairs carefully, because Mum wasn't keen on us carrying her up and down the stairs, and hunted in the kitchen, the sitting room, the downstairs loo, the tiny study and the hall. Mum was not in any of those places.

Bird appeared, blearily rubbing her eyes.

"Waz goin' on?"

"Can't find Mum," I said. I showed her the earring and her eyes widened.

"Have you looked outside?"

"No."

We stared at each other.

"What if she's in the Mob?" I whispered.

Ella stopped crying, burped, and grabbed my nose.

"What if she's seen Mister Rob again?"

"I'll go," said Bird. "You warn Stevie." I went to give her Ella but she shook her head.

"What are you going to say?" I asked.

"I have no idea," said Bird as she stepped out of the back door.

Me and the baby waited and waited and waited and waited and waited. I looked at Ella and she pointed to her mouth.

"Mum will be here in a minute," I told her. "She'll get your breakfast."

"Gass-min," said Ella.

There was a thud and Stevie landed in the room.

"What's happening?" he said, jumping up and sitting on the table.

I explained about Mum and his mouth went into this perfect O shape. Which would have been funny if everything wasn't feeling a bit weird.

"RELAX," called Bird from the back door. "She's not in the Mob."

"That's not relaxing," I said. "Where is she?"

"Mister Rob wasn't in the Mob either," said Bird.

I took Ella through the house to the front door. It was unlocked. I looked at the driveway. Only Mum's Bloomers van was there.

"THE CAR'S GONE!" I shouted. I was feeling seriously freaky now. Had Mum driven off and left us too?

Ella took a fistful of my hair and pointed to her mouth with her other hand.

"She'll be back soon," I said. Something was wrong.

Even if Mum was fed up with us, she'd never leave Ella. She was crazy for the baby. She barely let her out of her sight.

Something on the driveway beeped and flashed. I went to pick it up, the cold summer wind blowing through my T-shirt. It was the baby monitor, the one that Mum clipped to her belt when Ella was asleep upstairs. Now it showed a small, grainy TV recording of the empty cot – empty, of course, because I had Ella in my arms.

Mum ALWAYS had this on her if she didn't have the baby.

I ran back to the others and held up the monitor for them to see.

Bird grabbed the phone and dialled Mum's number. We waited breathlessly.

"Voicemail," she said.

This was too weird.

"Let's go and ask Russell if he knows anything," said Stevie.

I didn't see how he could, but as we were running out of ideas, we belted to the Mob.

"Russell, do you know what has happened to Mum?" asked Stevie.

"MISTER ROB TOOK HER," replied Russell.

"What?" shrieked Bird.

"HE'S TAKEN HER AWAY TO MAKE HER HAPPY," said Russell. "JUST LIKE YOU ASKED."

```
chapters[33].title =
```
"Hunting Rabbits";

Central London

MI5.5 Officer Snow shouted in triumph and punched the air.

"AT LAST!"

Henderson, recently returned from a fruitless trip to the delivery driver's empty house, smiled nervously.

"At last, ma'am?"

"FINALLY I have an address!"

"What address is this, ma'am?"

"The WRONG address, you muppet! The address the rabbit hutch was NOT sent to."

"Rabbit hutch, ma'am?"

"OH, KEEP UP! Russell 1,000,000 was supposed to arrive at the army base, remember? Instead they received the rabbit hutch. I have the address of the person who wanted the hutch in the first place."

"Oh!" Henderson felt a flood of admiration for his boss. "How did you manage that?" He himself had found it impossible to get this information from the delivery company.

Officer Snow smirked. "I went on eBay and pretended to search for rabbit accessories! Anyone who is selling a rabbit hutch is probably also selling bowls, feeders, maybe even rabbits. I went through six thousand sellers before I finally hit on this one."

"You did all that, ma'am?"

"Well, not myself, obviously. I got one of the secretaries to do it. Oh, and a top hacker to look into everyone's selling history. And eventually we found the VERY hutch, sold by a Mrs Peabody, two weeks ago, for three pounds and fifty-six pence, to an individual in Birmingham."

"What's his name?" asked Henderson. "Who is this person who is now harbouring the most powerful, expensive and deadly machine in the world?"

"A Mr O Fugue," said Snow. She sat at her desk and read her screen. "His previous purchase history includes three sets of football boots, a book about baby elephants, AND" – she looked meaningfully at Henderson – "twelve old PC motherboards and five metres of high-spec cabling. Plus reclaimed optic fibre and twelve portable solar panels."

"Who is this guy?" asked Henderson.

Snow smiled grimly. "Wait until you hear this. Only last week he ordered three pairs of ladies' giant knickers."

"Really? That's a bizarre profile."

"He's an oddball, all right. And right now he's our number one suspect."

Officer Snow read the address on the screen.

Mr O Fugue
14, Snowdonia Way
Birmingham.

"Google Earth it!" she ordered.

Henderson tapped and scrolled in on the street.

"The house is PINK!" said Snow. "What kind of person paints their house pink? It looks like a sunset on the Indian Ocean!"

"More like a pink gin fizz cocktail," supplied Henderson.

"And what is that EYESORE in the garden?"

"Looks like a mobile home, ma'am, and a kind of wind turbine?"

"And what are those enormous plants?"

"No idea, ma'am."

"Well, we've got him now. Send the helicopters at once. Arrest everyone on the premises and keep them in solitary confinement until we have got everything out of them."

"I'll just have to get an authorization from the Home Office and organize the helicopters with the RAF," Henderson said tentatively. There had been a lot of cuts and one couldn't just take off in helicopters any more. One had to get sign-off on everything. "We might be quicker if we just take the van."

"Whatever! Hurry up!" roared Snow.

"We'll be there before lunch, ma'am."

"Good, remember SOLITARY imprisonment for every single being at that address until I say otherwise."

"Of course, ma'am." Henderson hesitated. "And if there are children at the address, ma'am? Are they to be kept in solitary imprisonment also?"

"I SAID EVERY SINGLE PERSON," howled Snow.

```
chapters[34].title =
```
"Orphans";

Ella was crying. Everyone was shouting and nobody was taking any notice of her. She sat at the bottom of the Mob steps and tried to eat a slug.

"Why didn't you stop him?" Bird was yelling.

"HOW WOULD I STOP HIM?" asked Russell. "I COULDN'T STOP ANYTHING UNLESS YOU PUT ME IN THE DOORWAY."

"Where's our mum?" asked Stevie in a small voice. He'd only just stopped crying and his face was all blotchy.

"I DON'T KNOW," said Russell. "BUT THIS MAY HELP."

He whirred and blinked and a piece of paper shot out of him and wafted to the ground.

It was a page of code.

```
function makeMumHappy() implements
NoChildrenProtocol {

var cottage = airBnB.keywordLookup("Wales",
"Lake", "Mountains");

if (cottage.status == "available") {
cottage.book();

RUSSELL.print("£", 1000);
RUSSELL.print(clone);

self.google("How to drive a car");
self.setHumanSafetyLevel (MAXIMUM);
self.moveHuman("Mum", cottage);

}

}
```

###
###############

"I can't read that!" said Stevie, picking it up.

"I can." Bird took it and began scanning the page, line by line.

"IT IS A 'THOUGHT-LEAK' FROM MISTER ROB," said Russell. "I HAVE EMBEDDED A SECRET BUG IN HIM SO THAT PERIODICALLY HIS THOUGHTS WILL LEAK. I DO NOT KNOW WHEN THE LEAKS WILL OCCUR. I DID THIS AS A PRECAUTIONARY MEASURE." The printer fell silent.

"Well done," said Bird.

"What's happening?" asked Stevie.

"Every so often, Russell can read Mister Rob's mind," said Bird. "It comes out as printed code."

"What does it say?" I asked anxiously.

Bird screwed up her face. "Hmm, it's a mixture of C++ and Java. Let me see … it's called "Make Mum Happy". Oh, man!" Bird read on. "With NO children. Charming. There's something about booking a cottage in Wales via Airbnb. Crikey." Her mouth dropped. "And he's made Russell print one thousand pounds!"

"You can print money!" I yelped. "WOW. Why didn't we think of that?"

Bird stood in her tie-dyed splotchy pyjamas, levering herself up and down on her toes and chewing her hair.

"This next bit says Mister Rob is going to download driving instructions!"

"I don't like the sound of that," said Stevie.

"And this," pointed out Bird, "means he is going to take Mum away from here. Oh, my god!" Her voice wobbled. "He's actually taking her to Wales!"

My legs went all shaky and I flopped into the armchair. I remembered the talk we'd had about making Mum happy.

"How did he know to take her to Wales?" asked Bird.

Mum was always saying she wanted to go back to the mountains and sleep and eat and...

"I remember!" I said. "She was looking through photos when Mister Rob was destroying Stevie's room. She talked about it then. He *must have heard*."

Mister Rob must have phenomenal powers to hear Mum saying that, over the noise of him clearing up. And if he'd heard that, he must have heard EVERYTHING we said. I shivered. Mister Rob was way more creepy than I'd thought.

Stevie threw his hands over his face and burst into fresh tears. "First Stinky Elephant, now Mum," he whimpered.

"Look at this," said Bird, patting him on the shoulder and pointing to the code.

```
self.setHumanSafetyLevel(MAXIMUM);
```

"It means he is going to keep Mum safe."

Stevie sniffed. "He'd better."

"I'm trying to work out if we should phone the police," Bird said. "If we do, they will find out about Russell and Mister Rob and we could get into big trouble."

I looked out of the door at our empty Mum-less and Dad-less house. Weren't we in enough trouble already?

"Also we're temporary orphans," Bird said. "The

police might give us to the council to look after and then we won't be able to rescue Mum."

"They might split us up," said Stevie hugging Ella so close she burped. "They might put me on a farm, like what happened in the Second World War and I'd have to pull up turnips all day."

"They might send Ella to Australia to start a new life with an outdoorsy couple," I said. "People in clean shorts who would take her hiking and cook wild lizards. We might never see her again."

"They have crocodiles in Australia," said Stevie, shuddering.

"But the police would look for Mum," mused Bird. "They would use street cameras, internet booking sites, road cameras and all sorts to help find her."

"I CAN HELP WITH THAT," said Russell suddenly. "I HAVE FITTED MISTER ROB WITH A TRACKER. I CAN FIND HIM."

"Oh, wow," said Bird. "So you'll be able to pinpoint exactly where he goes?"

"YES," said Russell. "RIGHT NOW HE IS NORTH OF CHEPSTOW ON THE A48."

"We can do this ourselves. No one is taking Ella to Australia," said Stevie, sounding fiercer than he ever had.

"We should leave now," said Bird. "Before we get caught here alone."

"GOOD IDEA," said Russell.

"The thing is," said Bird, drumming her fingers on him, "we need to take you with us."

What? My sister was crazy. Russell wasn't exactly portable. It had taken two huge men and a van to get him here.

"He weighs a tonne," I said. "How will we get him on the bus?"

"We can't go by bus," said Bird.

"We can't bike there – it's too far. And what about Ella?"

"Let me think," said Bird.

In the silence, I thought of Mum and how worried she must be. I had to rub my eyes with my sleeve.

"We could load Russell into the van," said Bird.

"WHAT MAKE IS IT?" asked Russell excitedly.

"IF IT IS DIGITIZED I COULD DRIVE IT FOR YOU."

"Mum's van is twenty years old. It's definitely not digitized. It's barely motorized," said Bird. "I'll have to drive."

"You want to drive it to Wales?" I asked my sister, incredulous.

"Olly, our mum has been kidnapped by a mad robot," said Bird. "Of course I should drive."

Outside, Ella made a rude noise in her nappy area.

"You change it," Bird told me. "I'm thinking."

"I'm thinking too!" I protested. I hate changing nappies. I always end up with poo on my knees or in my hair.

"I'll do it," said Stevie reluctantly. "But you must both pay me five pounds."

"Two," said Bird.

"Three," said Stevie.

"Done," said Bird.

"I'm not paying him three pounds to change Ella's nappy," I protested.

"You change it then," said Stevie.

I noticed a brown-yellow line seeping through Ella's babygro.

"I'll pay," I said quickly.

"While you're at it, give her some Weetabix," said Bird. "No one fed her this morning."

We all paused.

"But she usually feeds FROM MUM in the morning," I said awkwardly, pointing to my chest.

"Oh, flip," said Bird. "I'd forgotten."

Ella spent half her life nestled up Mum's jumper, eating. How on earth were we going to look after her?

"Give her some Weetabix and warm up some milk from the fridge," said Bird.

When Stevie left, carrying the smelly, protesting baby, Bird stood close to Russell and glared into his lens.

"How did Mister Rob take Mum away?"

Russell's green light blinked.

"I DID NOT SEE OR HEAR. BUT I THINK SHE WAS VERY TIRED AND CONFUSED."

I was glad Stevie hadn't heard that bit.

"He didn't hurt her, did he?" I asked, feeling new tears form in my eyes.

"OF COURSE NOT, HURTING PEOPLE DOES NOT MAKE THEM HAPPY," retorted Russell.

Bird squeezed my arm. "We'll find her," she told me. She walked to the workbench and started fiddling with a pair of pliers.

"STUPID ROBOT," she said. Then she banged Russell hard on his side.

"Can you print a trolley that would hold your weight?" she asked "Which turns into a ramp?"

"I'll NEED A DIAGRAM," said Russell. We watched the screen as it scrolled through the internet, finally landing on a plan of a wheeled trolley with an adjustable ramp and a push bar.

"OFF I GO!" said Russell, and started printing.

The trolley was made of a hard, grey plastic, and it took thirty minutes for Russell to print and twenty minutes for us to slot together. During this time Stevie packed a carrier bag full of anything nice to eat he could find in the food cupboard and some clothes for the baby.

I walked back and forth, unloading boxes of Mum's pants from the van (hoping the neighbours weren't suspicious) and stacked them in the Mob where they reached the roof. I snagged my arm AGAIN on that blimmin' nail and had to tie a sock around it to stop the bleeding.

With a lot of shoving and arguing, we finally got Russell out of the Mob and on to the trolley, then along the path and into the van. It was a snug fit. As soon as he was stationary, Russell's solar panel extended out the window.

"JUST KEEPING THINGS CHARGED UP," he said.

It was nearly lunchtime before we were all sitting in the van. Ella was strapped into her car seat in the front, looking confused. Bird sat at the wheel, her hands shaking slightly. I was terrified. This was crazy. But what else could we do? Piggy licked my ear nervously.

"Do you know how to drive this thing?" asked Stevie.

"Not really," said Bird, starting the engine.

Ella gave a squeal.

Bird shut her eyes. Then she turned the engine off.

Everyone went quiet.

"I can't do it," she said. "Mum would hate this. Especially with Ella in here."

I breathed out in relief. I hadn't wanted to let on that I was absolutely terrified of Bird's plan.

"You'd probably crash," said Stevie.

"It was a stupid idea," said Bird. "We need to think again."

So now we were back in the kitchen, sitting round the table, eating bread and jam and sipping tea. We all like tea. Even Ella enjoys the odd spoonful.

We'd left Russell in the van because we still planned to go and save Mum. We were just not sure how.

Ella had fallen asleep in her buggy and was gently snoring under her monkey blanket. I looked at her with envy. I'd like to be asleep now. We were all exhausted and were looking forward to the baked beans that were bubbling on the stove. It seemed wrong to eat when Mum was missing, but Bird said we must.

"Shall we leave Russell in the van and go and find Mum by bus?" asked Stevie.

"We have to take Russell with us," said Bird. "Or we won't know where Mum is."

"But how?" I asked. It was the question we had been wondering ever since Bird had *not* driven us away.

"Maybe we should just phone the police," said Bird. "I can't sit here and do nothing."

"No way," said Stevie, grabbing the handle of Ella's buggy. "They'll treat us like children!"

On the mantelpiece there was a photo of Mum holding Stevie when he was a baby. Mum is wearing a mad hat, like a fur trapper and laughing so hard you can see the tears glinting in her eyes.

At that moment I was so mad with Mister Rob I wanted to fight him.

There was a sudden sharp knocking on the door and I jumped and slopped tea over my jeans. Stevie scooped up the sleeping Ella and flew upstairs.

It was the sound we had all been dreading and expecting.

Were Russell's owners finally here?

chapters[35].title =

"No Longer Orphans";

Someone was banging on the door so hard that the coloured glass was wobbling. In the hallway Piggy went completely crazy, barking like he was facing down a ghost.

"Let them in before they break it down," said Bird, her eyes huge with worry.

I felt sick. Was it the SAS? Or was it social services? Both were terrifying. I saw a tall, dark shadow through the glass. Holding my breath, I opened the door. Piggy rushed out, wagging his tail.

"But it's you!" I said, bewildered and rooted to the door mat.

"Hello, Olly. Hello, Piggy."

Stevie and Ella peeked down the stairs.

"DADDA!" squealed Ella.

Our dad stood there, our real dad, dressed in a new blue coat.

My first thought was, *Phew.* My second was, *No way!* My third was, *How come he looks SO OLD?*

I later realized this was because Russell had lopped five years from Dad's age when Mister Rob was being printed and had left out all major wrinkles.

"Are you OK?" asked Dad.

Now, when someone asks you if you are OK, normally you say "Yes", even if you've lost the football match, have a bad stomach ache and your shoes are pinching your toes off.

No one says "No" to that question, do they?

But I absolutely could not answer "Yes". Because here was Dad! Back after being GONE for approximately two months! And also because Mum had been Mum-napped by a crazy Dad-bot and left us with the baby.

"I've been better," I said finally. (What should I tell

him? Everything? Nothing? What, what, what?) But then I stopped thinking because I found myself hugging him, and even though his coat was new, I smelled Dad-smells of coffee and fog and then he lifted me right up, like he hadn't done for years and kissed my head.

"I've missed you," he said. "Really badly."

A tear fell down my cheek as Stevie belted out of the door, nearly knocking Dad over.

"What the heck happened to you?" sobbed Stevie from the folds of Dad's coat.

Dad mumbled something.

Bird stood on the bottom stair, holding Ella. Her face was expressionless. For once, it seemed, she had nothing to say.

"Hello, darling," Dad said.

Bird nodded once and tightened her grip on Ella.

Dad let go of Stevie (who did not let go of him) and cleared his throat.

"Where's Mum? She's not answering her phone."

We all three swapped a look.

"Can you fetch her, please?" said Dad, lingering on the doorstep.

"Come in," I said, pulling at his coat. "Please."

"I'd rather wait for your mum to say that," said Dad.

But me and Stevie dragged him in and firmly shut the door behind us. Dad wiped his feet and then took his shoes off anyway. He glanced around nervously, as if he expected Mum to appear at any minute. He was wearing odd socks. I liked that.

"What have you done to your arm?" asked Dad. The blood had seeped through and turned the sock black.

"The nail in the Mob," I said. "It has a thirst for human blood."

"I'll take it out," said Dad.

"No turnips now!" I said to Stevie, who was doing a snotty little happy crying thing. "No cooked lizards for Ella."

Dad looked very uncomfortable.

"Mum won't want me just walking in like this," he said.

"She's not here." Bird had finally found her voice.

"Where is she? In the garden?"

Nobody said anything.

"Wren, what's going on?"

"Wren" is Bird's real name. She hardly ever uses it. She still seemed to be struggling to talk, so me and Stevie pulled Dad into the sitting room, which was odd, because normally we would sit and chat in the kitchen. We were sort of treating him like a guest. Before he'd even sat down, Stevie blurted it out.

"Mum's been kidnapped!"

Now imagine you were us and you had to explain to your dad (of whom you felt a bit shy because you hadn't seen him for ten weeks) that your mum had been stolen away by a robot that had been built by a Super Printer.

Well, that's what we did.

Dad listened to the whole thing, his face growing more and more incredulous by the minute. Afterwards, he made us go through it again. I couldn't stop staring at him. He was definitely real because his front tooth was slightly wonky and his fingernails were all different lengths. I thought how Mister Rob wanted to be PERFECT. But the things that would have made him PERFECT were the things that made Dad IMPERFECT.

"So where is the printer now?" Dad was saying

"In Mum's van," said Stevie. "We need to take him with us because of the thought-leaks." Stevie kept stroking Dad's hair, like he was a cat.

"The what?"

I explained about Mister Rob's secret built-in leaker. I also mentioned the tracker.

When we were done, Dad took Stevie on his lap and gave him a cuddle.

"Are you sure this is real? You're not making it up?"

We all stared at him. Of course he didn't believe us. Who would?

"Mum has been kidnapped by this robot?" Dad took my hand. "Really, Olly?"

I nodded.

"We're going to find her one way or another," said Bird. "And you're not going to stop us."

"Why on earth would I stop you?" asked Dad. "I'm going to help you."

I was so relieved that I let out a funny sob-noise. I think I was worried Dad wouldn't want to help. And that would have broken my heart.

Bird tapped her fingers loudly on the door frame.

"Good. You can start by changing Ella's nappy. It's leaked again." Briskly she handed over the baby.

Dad, however, was so pleased to hold her that he couldn't help smiling.

"Hurry UP," shouted Bird.

She was far ruder to him than she'd ever been before. But Dad didn't seem to notice.

"Of course, you're right," he said, getting to his feet.

chapters[36].title =
"Crisps and Fizzies";

When Dad saw Russell in the back of the van, he whistled.

"WOW," he said. "WOW, WOW, WOW."

"HELLO, MR FUGUE," said Russell. "WE MEET AT LAST."

He was about to say something else but Bird slammed shut the van door.

"No time for chit-chat."

Me, Stevie and Ella went in the back and Bird sat in the front, with Piggy on the floor under her feet.

Bird didn't look at Dad once, unlike me and Stevie, who couldn't take our eyes off him. I think Stevie almost wanted to *eat* him.

"She's grown so much," said Dad, strapping Ella into her car seat and dropping a kiss on her head.

"What a surprise," muttered Bird.

"I HAVE AN UPDATE," said Russell. "MISTER ROB HAS STOPPED IN A SMALL PLACE CALLED LLANBEDR. IT IS IN THE BLACK MOUNTAINS."

"Why has he taken her *there*?" asked Dad.

"To make her happy, unlike you," retorted Bird.

I really didn't like the way my sister was talking to Dad. She would NEVER EVER have got away with this behaviour before. Dad said nothing, though. He just looked sad.

"He was trying to grant our wish to make Mum happy," explained Stevie. "He was a wish-granting robot."

Dad sighed.

Then we were off, out of the wilds of the city and down, down the M5 to the border.

*

The unmarked black car drew up and parked outside the pink house. A second, identical vehicle pulled in behind it. Two, three minutes passed, then as a man in the front seat raised his hand, three men swept out of each car and ran, fast and low, through the garden gate and up the short driveway. The six men were all dressed in black, wearing balaclavas and carrying automatic rifles.

Two men kicked in the front door and charged inside. The rest went round the back. A three-legged cat watched them lazily from its hiding place under a giant rhubarb plant. The men pushed open the door of a mobile home and entered.

Henderson, the man in the front seat, bawled into his phone.

"It MUST be in there."

Then as he listened, his face turned an unhealthy red.

"You found *what* in the boxes? KNICKERS? KNICKERS? WHAT ARE YOU TALKING ABOUT?"

*

It was over an hour before we stopped. Dad coming home had made us all mute as peanuts. Every so often he'd start to say something, then shut his mouth. I guess he didn't know where to start. What do you say to your kids when you have been gone for ten weeks? To be honest I was more worried about Mum than about asking him all the questions I would have asked if he had turned up this time yesterday.

Then Stevie said he needed the loo and Ella had woken up and was grizzling in her car seat, so we stopped at a service station near the Welsh border.

"Crisps and fizzies?" asked Dad.

"YES, PLEASE!" squealed Stevie.

Usually when we stop at a service station we beg for crisps and fizzy drinks and the answer is always NO, and we get water and apples instead.

"I'll have water, thanks," said Bird stiffly. "Sucking up to us won't make us forgive what you did."

"I guess not," said Dad, getting out.

"It will make ME forgive," said Stevie. "Barbecued beef flavour, please."

"You don't need to be so mean to him," I said, unclipping Ella and bouncing her on my knee.

"Yes, I do," said Bird.

When Dad came back he had apples, water, crisps and fizzies AND nappies and bottles of ready-made baby milk. He took Ella and tried to feed her but she kept her mouth shut and stared at him suspiciously.

"She's not used to having bottles in the day-time," explained Bird. "She feeds off Mum. Remember?"

Dad shrugged helplessly.

"Oh, no," said Stevie. "I heard that if cows don't get milked they, like, explode. Will Mum explode?"

"Mum is not a cow," said Bird. She handed Dad her bottle of water. "Give her some sips of this."

Ella drank a big gulp of water and immediately started coughing and spat it all over Dad's trousers.

"Oh, give her HERE," snapped Bird and took the baby from him.

We were all quiet, except the sound of eating and slurping and burping. (That was from Stevie – fizzies always made him burp.)

Dad cleared his throat. "I'm so sorry."

I held a crisp midway from the bag to my mouth.

"That's OK," said Stevie. "Let's go and rescue Mum."

Bird wasn't quite so forgiving.

"Where have you been?" she asked. "Why couldn't you come and see us?"

Dad moved round in his seat to face us.

"I've been staying in a hotel on the other side of the city."

"BUT WHY LEAVE US?" demanded Bird. "And why only the two phone calls?"

"Work things have been complicated, and me and your mum have been having some problems."

We knew this already.

"I was trying to work some things out," said Dad. "I did try and phone more, but you are out a lot."

"So lame," said Bird. "You didn't answer our calls or texts."

"Sorry," said Dad. "I really am. I've kind of been in hiding."

"From us?" asked Stevie.

"No … I…"

"Have you properly split up then?" interrupted Bird. I wished she hadn't asked that question because I did not want to know the answer.

"No, no," said Dad. "I just needed some space."

"You sent the drone!" I said. In all the chaos I'd completely forgotten. "You've been spying on us!"

"I wanted to check you were OK," said Dad. "It seemed like a good idea at the time."

"Then why didn't you ring or email or come and visit instead of sending that thing?" demanded Bird. "It freaked Mum right out. She thought she had a stalker. How could you abandon us?" She swallowed and buried her face in Ella's back.

"He's not abandoned us any more," said Stevie brightly. "No turnips for us, remember?"

Bird passed Ella back to Dad and got out of the car.

"Where are you going?" I asked.

"To give Piggy some air and see Russell."

"Look, I'm sorry about the drone. I was desperate to see you. I got it wrong…"

Bird slammed the door. Dad rubbed his face and Stevie handed him the box of tissues Mum always keeps in the front of the van. Then we were quiet for a bit. Even Ella.

"Dad, can I ask you something?" I swallowed.

"Of course."

"Are you going to vanish again?"

Dad turned round, his eyes were puffy. "No, I promise, not like that. Me and Mum need to talk properly and there are some work things that need to be looked at, but I promise I'll never disappear like that again. I made a mistake. I was very stupid and selfish."

"Hmmm." I folded my arms.

Bird came back, very quiet. She passed Piggy to me, who immediately licked my face and covered it with dog spit.

"I've got the address," Bird said. "Russell printed me a map. We're thirty-nine miles away. Let's go."

Dad reached for the map and Bird handed it over with extreme reluctance.

"Thanks," he said.

"LET'S GO," said Bird again.

We set off on to the misty motorway, with Ella grumbling more and more with every mile

"Shush, baby, shush," said Dad, and we all froze. We hadn't heard Dad say that for ages and we used to hear him say it every day.

"If Mum tries to give Mister Rob an order, will it work?" asked Stevie.

"No, Russell only imprinted our voices, remember?" Bird rested her knees on the back of Dad's seat and plugged in her iPod.

"What's that?" asked Dad, between shushings.

We explained about how Mister had tried to grant wishes for us and how these wishes had gone wrong.

"Such as?" asked Dad.

We told him about the bedroom-clearance disaster and the talking-dog episode.

"And how we narrowly avoided him intercepting two transatlantic planes to stop it raining!" said Stevie, laughing.

"What?"

"He is a pretty sophisticated robot," I said.

Dad was looking very alarmed indeed.

"What did you program into the printer? Where are the plans? What does this robot look like?"

"Ahh," I said. "It's interesting you should mention that." Then I realized that nobody had told Dad the robot looked exactly like him and decided to explain later. What was the rush?

chapters[37].title =

"Holiday Home";

I must have fallen asleep because one minute I was staring out of the window at the blurry scenery and thinking how, from the outside, we must look like an ordinary family, and how far that was from the truth. The next minute, I opened my eyes and found myself in a valley surrounded by mountains.

"We're here," said Bird.

Everyone was awake, even Ella, who had a serious look on her face.

"Shall we go and get Mummy, Ella?" whispered Stevie.

We were driving down a stony little lane with

hordes of pink flowers in the hedges, which seemed to be cheering us on. We arrived at a gate with a stone fox on either side, and after driving through, we came to a wide lake and a little grey cottage, tucked under the mountain.

"*Pen Y Fan*," said Bird. "The end of the road."

The cottage was like something out of a magazine. It was very old, made of stone, with black-painted windows, slates on the roof and a massive chimney. The mountain rose up steeply behind and was dotted with sheep. I could see no other houses.

I couldn't think too much about the nature stuff, though. All I wanted was Mum, safe and back with us.

Dad turned off the engine. You could almost hear the silence.

"Now what?" I asked.

"Let me go," said Dad. "You all stay in the car."

"No, I'm not..." began Bird, then stopped as the cottage door opened. Piggy growled and put his tail between his legs as Mister Rob came out. Everyone gasped, except Dad, who swore. Mister Rob looked at us, clocked Dad, and then disappeared round the back of the house. He still had the tea cosy on his head.

"That's the robot?" said Dad in a choking voice.

"Yes," said Bird.

Piggy wouldn't stop growling.

"But it's me," said Dad. "Why does he look like me?"

He got out of the car. "Wait here," he ordered and he ran towards the house.

"I'm not waiting…" said Bird. Then Mister Rob was back and he was heading straight for Dad. I started to panic. Mister Rob was so much tougher and stronger than Dad. What if he hurt him?

"YOU DO NOT MAKE MUM HAPPY!" roared Mister Rob.

"WHAAT?" Dad roared back. "Where is she?"

Dad had slammed into Mister Rob like a mad sumo wrestler and, amazingly, Mister Rob went flying.

"He's down!" screeched Stevie.

"He's up," remarked Bird, as Mister Rob rolled to his feet like a gymnast and spun to face Dad.

"WHERE IS MY WIFE?" howled Dad. He started

towards the cottage but Mister Rob was blocking his way.

"You cannot go in. You do not make her happy."

"How do you know?" shouted Dad flustered. "Why do you look like me? What's going on?"

"According to her diary, you have made her sad on at least thirty-five occasions over fifteen years," said Mister Rob, who had shot out a hand and was gripping Dad's shoulder.

He kind of reminded me of Darth Vader at that moment.

"Mister read Mum's diary," said Bird. "That's low."

"That's not too bad," yelped Dad. "Did you count how many times I made her happy?"

"She did not record that data," replied Mister Rob. As we watched, somehow unable to move, Mister twisted Dad on to the floor and sat on his head. Mister was A LOT tougher than our dad.

Dad was squirming around, which wasn't very nice to see.

I opened my door.

"STOP IT," I yelled.

But Stevie was already there, booting Mister in the shins.

"LEAVE HIM ALONE."

"It's all right," said Bird. "He's programmed to NOT hurt humans. Not badly anyway."

"It looks like dodgy coding to me." I scrambled out of the car.

"He does not make her happy," Mister was saying.

"Where is our mum?" I demanded.

"I am still trying to fulfil your wish," said Mister Rob, clamping a firm hand on Dad's leg.

"It will make her happy to see us," said Stevie.

"Really?" said Mister in surprise. **"But you are small, noisy children who argue with her all the time."**

"It's illogical but it's true. She still loves us despite those things," said Bird, who had finally joined us. "Can you get off my father's head now?"

"Love again," sighed Mister. **"It always trips me up."** He stood and pulled our rather crumpled-looking Dad to his feet.

"Is she in there?" Dad gasped, pointing to the cottage.

"Yes," said Mister. **"She is not happy yet."** He still had a tight grip on Dad's arm.

"You can't make her happy," said Dad wearily. "But I think I can."

"Oh, per-lease," groaned Bird. "As if."

"I have another plan," said Mister. **"I will fulfil your wish by another method."**

He let go of Dad and stood back.

Pushing past, we all flew to the door of the cottage. I was about to go in when I felt a hand on my shoulder. Dad stood, panting.

"Let me go first," he said. "Really."

"We'll go in together," I said firmly.

The corridor floor was made of slippy slate and the place smelled of sheep. Mum's coat was hanging on a peg. A funny noise came out of my throat when I saw it.

I heard a muffled banging coming from the back of the house. We passed a sitting room, which was so tidy it looked like no one had ever lived in it, and on the other side was a small dark kitchen. A plate of cold pie sat, untouched, on the counter.

"Mum?" I called.

The banging was coming from behind a door at the end of the corridor.

"MUM?" shouted Stevie.

The key was in the lock.

I turned it, but Dad opened the door and stepped in first.

"OH, GO AWAY, YOU FREAK!" screamed Mum's voice. "THIS IS NOT MAKING ME HAPPY! I NEED MY CHILDREN TO BE HAPPY! I NEED TO BE FREE TO BE HAPPY! I NEED MY BABY TO BE HAPPY! NOT YOU! YOU HEAP OF JUNK!"

"Jasmine, it's really me," said Dad softly.

"Let me out, you dumb MACHINE," roared Mum. "I AM UNHAPPY, YOU CRAZED INSTRUMENT!"

I barged into the room.

Mum stood, her face red and her eyes swollen. Her hair was sticking out everywhere and she was wearing her pink, flowery pyjamas and black farmer wellies.

I felt happier than I had ever been in my life.

"YOU!" screamed Mum, running to me and

knocking Dad completely over. She swept me up into a hug and carried me out of the room. It was like she was superhuman. Then she slammed the door shut and turned the key.

"SEE HOW YOU LIKE IT, METAL-HEAD!" she shouted. She set me down, kissed me, hugged me, and growled. She smelled bad, like a rugby captain on a hot day.

"WHERE ARE THE OTHERS? WHERE'S THE BABY?" Mum was sobbing and yelling at the same time.

"Mum, it's fine. We're here. Everyone's here," said Bird.

Mum grabbed Ella off Stevie and kissed everyone at once. Piggy just kept barking and barking like he knew it was an important moment.

"Gass-min!" said Ella in delight. She took a fistful of Mum's wild hair and would not let it go. Mum bundled us all along the corridor and out of the door.

"Mum, that really is Dad in there."

"No, he only looks like him. He's a machine. A clever, very STUPID machine."

"No, it really IS DAD."

"No, it is NOT."

Then everyone was talking at once so no one really knew what anyone was saying. I think Mum was asking how we had found her and Bird said, "Russell," and I think Mum thought there was some bloke called Russell who was good at finding people, but it was too much to explain in the moment. Instead I took an envelope out of my pocket, opened it and gave Mum the ruby earring that was inside.

"Oh, my darling," said Mum, and hugged me once again.

When there was a break in all the emotion, I spoke.

"Mum, you know, that really is Dad in that room." I thought he'd probably want to come out by now.

"No, sweetheart, it's a very sinister robot. I know it's hard to understand, but it is! Technology is so advanced these days."

"It is Dad," said Bird. "The robot is outside somewhere. Don't worry, he's harmless."

"Dad came back this morning," said Stevie. "We know all about the robot. We made him."

Mum paused. I could almost see the thoughts shooting past her eyes.

"Are you sure?" she said. "He was very lifelike. It would be easy for you to be fooled."

"Mum, think. The robot was wearing a checked red shirt, yes?" Bird smiled. "Dad was wearing his bad green jumper."

"I don't remember what he was wearing," said Mum. "I didn't look too closely at him."

She clutched my hand.

"Don't let him out. He's a very, very clever robot."

We all groaned.

Bird explained again about Dad coming home and us coming to rescue her, but it didn't seem to sink in. Mum looked very dazed, like she had been up all night. Actually she probably had been up all night. She couldn't seem to believe that the real Dad was really here.

"Go and talk to him," said Stevie. "Then everything will be clear."

"Machines can be cunning," said Mum. "He might have just changed his clothes."

She stroked Ella's cheek.

"OK, everyone get in the car. Bird, you go in the driver's seat. If I run out and shout, "DRIVE," you just drive everyone away to safety and call the police. If I'm not out in ten minutes, drive anyway. OK? You drove around that field last year. Can you remember how to do it?"

"Not really," said Bird and gave me a look.

"Just do it," said Mum. She kissed Ella tenderly, squeezed Stevie's shoulder and went back into the house.

"IT'S DAD!" we all shouted, exasperated.

Of course we didn't sit in the car as instructed. Instead, after a few minutes, we crept up to the thick, studded door and listened. Stevie had Piggy and I held Ella close. Would Dad be able to convince her he was human?

"SO," called Mum through the door. "WHO ARE YOU?"

"Jasmine, it's me, Oscar," answered Dad. "I'm your husband. I'm so sorry."

"WHAT'S MY MIDDLE NAME?" demanded Mum.

"What? Oh, I see. Look, Jas, it really is me. You haven't seriously got me mixed up with a machine, have you?"

(Silence.)

"Just do it, Dad," Stevie muttered to himself.

"OK, OK, it's Anna."

"WHEN IS OUR WEDDING ANNIVERSARY?"

(Silence.)

"The tenth of June. No, no, no, I mean the twelfth. Sorry. I knew that."

"That's not a deal-breaker," whispered Bird. "That's normal behaviour."

"All right, what is the date of birth of our second child?"

"Oliver Jim was born on the first of January, eleven years ago," answered Dad. "In the living room, at nine o'clock at night, just after his older sister had fallen asleep. Now do you believe I am not a machine?"

"You could have found that information in my diary," said Mum. "I know you've been reading it, you sneak."

"Let me out, darling. You must be so tired. I know I am."

"OK, prove to me you are not a machine. Let's have a pretend conversation. You are a woman, pretending to be a man."

"What is she on about?" I asked Bird. "Has she gone nuts?"

"She's being scientific," said Bird. "Aping the Turing Test." She smiled. It was the first time I'd seen my sister smile for ages.

"What?"

"Shhhh"

"Hello, Jasmine, let's play football," said Dad in a falsely deep tone. "Or shall we go to the pub and talk about cars?"

"Very funny," said Mum. But something had changed in her voice.

"What did I want to be when I was twenty-one?" she asked.

"Am I still a woman?" asked Dad.

"ANSWER ME," snapped Mum.

"You wanted to be the clock mechanic for Big

Ben." Dad was still speaking in his extra-deep voice. "You also wanted to be a marine scientist specializing in seaweed. You also wanted to hold the world record for doing the splits while juggling strawberries."

"OK, Mr Know-it-all."

I grimaced when I heard the word "Mister".

"What is intelligence?"

(Pause.)

"These questions are too hard," complained Stevie, sitting on the doorstep. "Just get her to let him out."

"I don't feel intelligent enough to answer that properly now," Dad was saying. "But basically it's lots of neural networks finding solutions to a myriad of problems."

"IS THAT WHAT YOU'RE DOING NOW?"

"I've only got one problem in mind at the moment," said Dad. "I'm trying to convince my wife I'm not a machine."

"WHAT IS NOT COMPUTABLE?" asked Mum.

"Good question," murmured Bird. "Go, Mum."

There was a long silence then. There would have

been an even longer silence if I'd been trying to answer it.

"Love," said Dad. "How do you compute love? And I love you. Very much."

"Hmmm," said Mum. Then she called him a very rude word indeed.

"She MUST think it's Dad," whispered Stevie. "She only uses that word on him."

We heard nothing for a while because Mum stopped shouting and started whispering, and Ella was starting to grizzle so we crept back to the car. Five minutes passed. Ten minutes passed.

Stevie went to wee in the lake and Bird went for a chat with Russell, so only me and Ella saw Mum come out, followed by Dad.

They didn't look like they were a deeply-in-love sort of couple. For one thing, they weren't touching or even looking at each other. They were looking at ME. Also, Mum looked really, really, really MAD. Angry mad, not nuts mad. Still, they were in the same eyeshot, and that was a hundred per cent better than recent times.

Now would come a lot of explanations. I'd have to talk about rabbit hutches and 3D printers and robots and wishes and talking dogs. But as I opened my mouth, Dad said:

"I recognize this place. It's out of the holiday home brochure."

I *knew* I had seen it somewhere. Mum kept a brochure by the loo. She had been about holiday homes like I had been about rabbits. She dreamed very strongly.

"I'm cured of holiday homes," said Mum, taking Ella from me.

None of us wanted to go back in the house, so we settled on the damp ground and listened as Mum told her story.

Last night she had drunk some tea, and then she'd felt very, very sleepy. When she'd woken up, she'd been in the car. She still felt very tired and when she looked over, half-asleep, she'd seen Mister Rob, who at first she'd thought was Dad. She thought she was still dreaming and had gone back to sleep and when she had woken again, she found herself here, in the living room of the house.

She was very confused, of course, and when Mister appeared, she had become very frightened, even though he didn't hurt her and was trying to be kind. Mister kept saying, "BE HAPPY! WHY WON'T YOU BE HAPPY?"

"It's all been very strange," said Mum. "Perhaps you could tell me what's been going on, for real this time?"

A secret service van, Sainsbury's car park, Wolverhampton

"We've had a satellite image of Vehicle X at a remote cottage in the Welsh Black Mountains," called Henderson from his office in the back of his van.

"Send the helicopters immediately," said M15.5 officer Snow into her headset. "We've got everything to lose." She paused. "If this doesn't work, we will have to enable the remote programming device. We can't risk Russell going overseas."

"What remote device, ma'am?" asked Henderson, pressing his phone to his ear to hear better.

Snow paused. "The self-destruct program."

Henderson gasped. "What?"

"Oh, yes," said Snow. "If Russell is not returned to us, we can enable the function that will turn it into a bomb in a matter of minutes, EVEN if we don't know its exact location."

"Isn't that rather dangerous, ma'am?" gulped Henderson. "I'm sure we'll have it very soon."

"Russell is getting too close to the sea," hissed Snow. "In as little as an hour it could be on a speedboat and out of our waters. You DO NOT understand how deadly it is."

"But a bomb, ma'am? Is that ethical?"

"Listen, you twit. Nobody, except me and the head of the program, knows about this function. Even the people who MADE Russell do not know about it. It was coded in deep secrecy. Therefore, if it explodes, no one will know it was deliberate."

"OK, ma'am." Henderson ended the call. He wondered sometimes if his boss was a little bit crazy. Then he looked at the group of burly soldiers squeezed into the van next to him.

"Let's go," he ordered.

chapters[38].title =
"Dad Comes Clean";

Mum and Dad were still talking, so us kids and Piggy wandered along the shoreline. There were some big black-and-white geese splashing around further out, and the ground was all trampled by webbed feet and dotted with goose poo. The sun glinted off the water and far away, on the other side of the lake, a red post van glided silently along the road. The only noise was a tiny drone of a silvery plane hundreds of metres up in the sky, the odd echoing goose honk, and the murmuring of our parents.

I was REALLY hungry.

"Do you think they'll get back together?" I said,

nodding at them. Mum was waving her arms around, her pyjamas billowing in the breeze.

"Maybe," said Bird.

"I wish they'd hurry up. I want my lunch," I said. How long did it take to make up, anyway?

I skimmed a stone over the water. My record was twelve hops. Stevie's was five.

"I'd say there's a fifty-fifty chance of them coming home together," said Bird. "Mum still looks pretty narked."

"'Course they will," said Stevie. "I told them to."

Bird went to check on Russell. We heard the van door open, then the sound of paper rustling.

"Oh, man," said Bird to herself. "What now?"

I bit into an overripe orange. I hoped it wasn't anything that would hold up dinner.

"Mister Rob had another thought-leak." My sister appeared round the side of the van. She held out a new page of code. "It doesn't make sense."

"Ha!" I said. "That's how I feel when I look at code!"

*

Mister Rob's thought-leak:

```
##########################################
##############

function makeMumHappy2() {

self.moveToLocation(37.7749300, -122.4194200);

var virus = generateHappyMumVirus();

MAZZO.addPlayer("MISTER ROB");
MAZZO.disableProtocol(GlobalData
Security);

foreach (player in MAZZO) {
player.addToZone("MISTER ROB");
    player.addToOxygenPoints(virus);

if (player.warningOfDataLoss) {
ignoreWarning();
}
```

}

}

\#
\#\#\#\#\#\#\#\#\#\#\#\#\#\#

Bird was muttering to herself. "HappyMumVirus? What the heck is that?"

She stopped as Mum and Dad wandered over *together*. Not lovey-dovey together, but still walking as a team, a unit, a pair.

"What's that?" asked Dad.

"Nothing you'd understand," answered Bird rudely. Mum looked like she was about to say something, then changed her mind.

"Why does it say MAZZO here?" I pointed.

"I don't know yet," said Bird. "But I think it's bad. He's MOVED somewhere. These are the GPS coordinates."

"It's another thought-leak," Stevie told our parents.

"Let me see," said Dad.

"You don't understand code," said Bird.

Dad bit his lip.

Mum looked very, very tired. She'd opened the front door of the van and was sitting inside, feeding Ella. Stevie got in next to her and put his little hedgehog head on her shoulder.

"Show him the code," Mum ordered.

Bird snorted and handed it over.

Dad read the paper and pursed his lips. He needed a shave. He looked like a burglar.

"Oh, dear," he said. He touched Bird's shoulder and she jumped like she'd been electrocuted. "Can you help me with this?"

Bird shrugged, picked up a stone and threw it in the direction of the lake. It clattered on the shore and Piggy scampered after it.

"Please," said Dad.

Bird took back the page.

"This bit is about MAZZO," she said. "But the first line is *still* about making Mum happy."

"Oh, lord," said Mum from the van. "No more making me happy. Please!"

"What has MAZZO got to do with making Mum happy?" I asked.

Bird looked at Dad. "You can understand it, can't you? I can see it in your face."

"I think so," said Dad. "He's saying he wants to hack into all MAZZO-users' accounts. He's going to do this by infiltrating the main MAZZO server..."

"And then upload himself," said Bird. "This bit." She pointed.

```
player.addToZone("MISTER ROB");
```

"Eh?" Stevie looked as puzzled as I felt.

"He's going to get into MAZZO," I explained. I paused. "Then what?"

"Then," said Bird, "he's going to unleash a massive virus, so strong it will destroy all of MAZZO."

```
player.addToOxygenPoints(virus);
if (player.warningOfDataLoss) {
ignoreWarning();
}
```

"This is quite bad," said Bird. "He's putting ALL the

players in the world in one game, then he's going to infect their oxygen points with the Happy Mum Virus."

"NO," shouted Stevie, so loud it made the baby sit up and look around.

"The next bit is very bad," said Dad. "It says to ignore a warning if all the players lose their data. That's not just MAZZO data, that's everything on their computers. Work, photos, emails, programs, everything."

"But why?" I asked.

Bird swallowed and pointed to a line of code at the top of the page.

"To make Mum happy."

"Oh, for GOODNESS' SAKE," said Mum.

"He must have overheard you moaning about MAZZO, Mum," I said.

"We HAVE to stop him," said Stevie.

All around us, everything was quiet. The breeze had dropped and the lake was still. I tried to imagine a world without MAZZO.

What would we do?

"Where is Mister Rob anyway?" I asked. "We'll just tell him not to do it."

But nobody knew where he was. We'd all been too pleased to see Mum to worry about him

"Look," said Bird, pointing to an empty space beneath a hedge.

"What?" I asked.

"Mum's Peugeot. It's gone."

So now we had a new problem on our hands.

"Let's see what Russell has to say," said Bird, flinging wide the back doors of the van. We all crowded round.

"Russell, where is Mister Rob?" asked Bird.

Russell printed a piece of paper.

123–456, Camarthan Way
 Mumbles
 The Gower

Dad took out his phone and Googled the address.

"It's SeaAcre," he said. "It's the biggest server farm in Europe and it belongs to MAZZO."

"What's a server farm?" I asked.

"It's usually a large building, like a warehouse with lots of servers," said Bird. "Servers, as you know, are machines that hold data. The servers can 'talk' to each other, so can compute much more data than just one machine. They're like a giant brain, capable of assimilating maybe fifty petabytes of information."

"Whoa," I said. "Mister Rob is, like, a cyber terrorist."

"Time to call in the professionals?" asked Mum.

"I AM the professionals," said Dad.

"You were sacked," said Mum.

I often hear conversations between my parents that I do not understand and this one was no different. So I was going to skate over it. But Bird had other ideas.

"Professional what? You used to work in science data research. You got the sack. For the last six months you've been unemployed. What's Mum talking about?"

"Going to come clean?" asked Mum.

"I am now," said Dad. He glanced at the van. "Let's go where it can't hear us."

"'It' is called Russell," I said, watching Dad. I like watching him. I love the way he scratches his nose. He does it with his little finger, the one you would least expect.

"How do you know Russell is listening?" questioned Stevie. "He looks asleep to me."

"He never sleeps," said Dad.

"How do you know?" asked Bird.

"Because I created him," said Dad.

Well! We were all dumbstruck. Flabbergasted. Amazed. Confused. Shocked and ... a bit frightened. At least I was.

Bird was the first to speak.

"Data?" she said.

This was Bird's way of asking Dad to explain himself.

The sound of a distant helicopter echoed through the mountains. It made the flock of geese on the other side of the lake rise up and fly into the air, honking and flapping

Dad looked uneasily into the sky.

"OK," he said. "But first, let's get out of here."

chapters[39].title =
"The Chase";

The helicopter beat down to land in front of the small, stone cottage. The lake water blew sideways in strange whirlpools and the small copse of trees billowed and lashed like they were in a hurricane.

The door of the aircraft flew open. Six figures in black jumped out, one after the other, and spread around the house. Within minutes they were inside and running through every room, checking every window.

A lone figure stood, his phone to his ear and growled in frustration as the men reported that no one was inside.

"Sir, we think they've only left recently. And we've just found something."

Henderson was handed a sheet of paper with what looked like computer code printed on it.

He squinted at the page, and even turned it upside down. Then he jabbed a number into his phone.

"GET ME A TOP CODER NOW!" he shouted.

chapters[40].title =
"SeaAcre";

This is what Dad told us, as we drove, drove, drove, out of the mountains.

Six months ago he was sacked from his job. We knew this already. What we didn't know was that instead of working as a science designer (whatever that was) at the university, he was actually sponsored by the British Space and Military Partnership. Which is a group of people who combine research into space and designing things, like army radars and rockets.

Anyway, Dad had been working on a top secret project for about five years, which is why he was so quiet about what he did. Even Mum didn't know all the details. And the project was … Russell.

Russell, Dad said, cost billions to make and was the latest, most up-to-date 3D printer in the world. But he wasn't just a printer, he was also a powerful computer, data recorder and analyst. He could track satellites, listen in on almost any digital conversation and print almost anything. (We knew that bit too.) Dad said he owned the intellectual rights to Russell, so he owned both the "idea" and final design of him.

"I see," I said, not seeing the teeniest bit.

"Why did you call him Russell?" asked Stevie.

"It's your mum's maiden name, the surname she had before she married me," said Dad, shooting her a sheepish look. "I thought it was a romantic gesture."

Mum snorted and Dad hurriedly continued with his story.

He'd grown worried, as Russell was being assembled, that he was going to be used for BAD THINGS. Like making guns, instead of parts for astronauts to use to fix space stations or medical equipment. Dad fell out with the bloke he was working with and then his office got broken into, and his contracts and legal documents concerning Russell were stolen.

Then he was sacked.

Dad looked really miserable when he was saying this bit. He said he'd got so involved in it all that he'd lost touch with his family, and he'd even missed Ella being born because he was at a meeting that he thought was more important.

He'd had an email from an old colleague four weeks ago, saying that Russell was going to be sent to the army to make weapons and Dad was so shocked, he and some friends had arranged for Russell to go missing.

"How very unlikely," said Bird.

"But not impossible," I replied.

Dad paused, like he had a whole massive story in his head he was wondering whether to tell us.

"It wasn't easy," he said. "And it was the wrong thing to do. I'd intended for it to be hidden somewhere else. But there is actually a whole secret team of us behind this and I still haven't worked out who is friend and who is foe. The machine was transported in secrecy under armed guard and somewhere along the line the whole thing got fouled up and Russell went missing!"

"I don't get it," said Stevie.

"I don't blame you," said my dad. "The timing was awful. It was just when me and Mum needed some time apart. I couldn't believe it when I heard, a few days ago, that instead of Russell being delivered to my lock-up, it was at my home address. One of my team completely messed up. I came as soon as I could."

"Did you know we had it?" I asked Mum.

"No," she said. "I've been too busy trying to keep everything going." She squeezed my arm.

Dad continued.

"I've been keeping an eye on you from a distance, I knew it was possible I was a suspect so I couldn't come home."

"The drones were horrible," said Bird. "We were really spooked by them."

"Sorry," said Dad. "I didn't think you would open the crate. After all, it was addressed to me."

"NO, it was addressed to me!" I protested.

"Why on earth would it have been addressed to you?"

"Because you are both Mr O Fugue," said Bird, somewhat wearily.

"Ahhh," said me and Dad, at exactly the same time.

"So you stole some technology," said Bird. "Will you go to prison?"

Dad looked away. "I don't think so. How can I steal what is mine?"

I felt confused. I was happy Dad was back, or back-ish anyway. But I was sad that he'd had all these secrets.

"Oh, come on ," said Bird. "Let's go and stop Mister Rob."

Mum was not wild about driving to The Gower to find Mister Rob, but she reluctantly agreed that if the whole world of MAZZO collapsed, along with ten billion people's personal data, all in the name of making *her* happy, that would be bad, so this might be worth a shot.

"It's my fault," she said. "I should have kept a closer eye on you all."

"No, it's my fault," said Dad. "I shouldn't have let Russell anywhere near my family."

"Oh, come on," said Bird.

My sister was being really cheeky but no one told her off.

So us kids and the dog were shunted to the back and our parents sat together in the front. After only ten minutes Mum was asleep.

"Put your foot down, Dad," ordered Bird. And he did, so we barrelled through the Welsh countryside, with hedges and green hillsides and little crumbling castles flashing past.

"What are we going to do when we get there?" asked Stevie, chewing through the garage pasty he had forced Dad to stop and buy, despite being mad with worry over MAZZO.

"Stop Mister Rob," said Bird, who had chosen a gherkin and hot pickle wrap. I was working my way through a sausage roll. Never had food tasted so delicious. Piggy sat at my feet and watched me lovingly, so I tore him off a bit.

"Mister Rob hasn't done anything yet." Bird removed her Headsetz. "I just checked my MAZZO account and it is all fine."

"Mister Rob ought to stop if we ask him," said Stevie

anxiously. "He's supposed to do what we say."

"He didn't do what I wanted," murmured Mum from the front. "I told him what would make me happiest was for him to go and jump in the lake. At least my Bloomers data is safe," she went on. "I never played the flipping game."

We three children went quiet.

"Actually, we DID sign you up ages ago," admitted Stevie. "We thought it would be a fun surprise."

"WHAT? So all my work is at risk?"

Bird nodded. "Yes. Your email, your spreadsheets, your customer lists, your factory payments, your knickers designs – everything."

"Let's go and DESTROY that blinking robot," fumed Mum.

We drove on with absolutely NO plan.

It was over two hours before we finally reached the town of Mumbles. Here, we stopped in a car park and we all went in a building marked "TY BYCHAN", which Mum said were the Welsh words for toilet.

When we came out, we couldn't find the van.

"That's it," said Stevie, pointing to a white van, identical to ours, but for the signs on the sides, which read:

THE BEST SANDWICHES IN THE UNIVERSE

"That's a sandwich van," said Dad

"So why is Mum inside?" Stevie raced over. He was right. Mum was sitting in the driver's seat. And the number plate was the same. It WAS our car. How had the sign changed?

Mum wound down the window.

"Quick, quick," she said.

When we were all bundled in the car, Mum screeched off very fast, following Dad's directions to SeaAcre, the server farm.

"This is so we can get in," explained Mum. "There was another van parked nearby, so I swiped its magnetic sign."

"It will never work," said Dad.

"That's stealing!" said Stevie, shocked.

"I promise I'll give it back," said Mum. She really was full of surprises.

We drove through the town, every now and then getting glimpses of the sea, round some roundabouts and finally we drew into a big industrial estate, with lots of large, grey, warehouse buildings.

"How's MAZZO?" Stevie asked Bird. She always got better wifi with her amazing Headsetz.

"Everything still OK," reported Bird. "The planet is calm. The Queen is handing out oxygen points."

"How are my Space Pups?" Stevie squinted at the tiny screen above Bird's ear. "Can you see Larry or Barry? Or Carrie?"

"Stay calm," said Bird. "Mister Rob hasn't uploaded himself yet."

We drove round the industrial estate. There were many different businesses: from a motorbike-fixing unit to a hairdressing-supplies centre. It was a maze of mown verges, signs, logos and tarmac roads.

"We're here," said Dad.

We'd left the main bit of the industrial estate and were parked alongside a tall, raggedy hedge. Tall metal gates sealed off the road. There was a large, white sign.

SEAACRE.

Through gaps in the hedge I saw the heaving, grey sea.

"Server farms are often on the coast," explained Bird. "They use the sea water to help keep things cool."

"There's Mum's Peugeot," pointed Dad. "It's parked on that little lane."

A guard in a black uniform started walking towards us.

"What now?" asked Bird.

"Don't worry," said Mum, winding down the window.

Everyone fell silent.

"Can I help?" asked the guard. His face looked like it had been beaten by the Welsh wind every day for fifty years. Deep frown lines were etched between his eyes. A walkie-talkie was clipped to his belt.

"Sandwiches," said Mum cheerfully.

"Why have you brought the family?" asked the guard, checking the sign on the side of the van. "Is that a dog?" He sneered at Piggy.

I did not like the man.

"My childcare let me down," said Mum.

The guard turned away and spoke into his walkie-talkie.

"That's done it," said Dad. "You should have let me show my university pass."

"Shhh, he's coming back," said Bird.

The guard marched up to the window. I looked desperately at the grey building ahead. How would we get to Mister Rob now?

"I'll have a cheese and pickle, and Fred, on the back gate, wants chicken tikka," said the guard.

"I'll see what I've got left on the way out," said Mum, firmly winding up the window. The guard stood back, clicked a button and the gates slowly opened.

"Mum, you are AMAZING," said Stevie.

"It's true," said Dad.

"I know," said Mum.

At first, the server farm looked just like any of the other huge warehouse-type buildings elsewhere on the estate. Then I noticed the big red doors with the MAZZO logo on them.

There were tall vents in the roof and, above these, the air wobbled like a heat haze.

"Where is everyone?" asked Stevie, as Dad pulled into the nearly empty car park.

"This place probably runs itself," said Dad, and I shivered.

"OK," said Bird. "Let's go and find that overgrown tin can."

We started unclipping our seat belts but Mum held up her hand.

"Wait here," she said. "This is a job for the grown-ups."

```
chapters[41].title =
```

"Snow Gives an Order";

The airfield was alive with helicopters taking off, one by one. Officer Snow couldn't help ducking as she ran under the rotating blades and clambered into the machine, even though she knew she was far too short to be at risk of injury.

According to the latest report, Russell was only minutes from the coast, and then, who knew?

She strapped herself into her seat and immediately dialled the number of the Prime Minister. Unfortunately she had discovered that he knew about the self-destruct button so she'd have to persuade him to use it.

"Sir, we need to abort the project immediately," she

yelled over the noise of the engine, as the door was slammed shut and the machine began to rise. "We will not reach the coast in time. We must destroy this machine before it goes offshore."

She listened to the raving voice on the other end of the line. The Prime Minister was not happy. He didn't want billions of pounds of technology going up in smoke, but nor could he risk it falling into enemy hands. And when Snow switched off her phone, she breathed out in relief.

She spoke into her headset.

"Activate the self-destruct. I repeat, activate the self-destruct." She paused. "YES, EXPLODE THE MACHINE NOW!"

Officer Snow settled back in her chair and watched the landscape gliding below.

She would arrive in time to see the smoke.

chapters[42].title =

"HappyMumVirus";

"MUM," exploded Bird. "We've got to stop Mister. He wants to destroy MAZZO."

"I know," said Mum. "That's why we're here. But he might try and kidnap you too."

I made a note NOT to bring my mother with me next time I'm tracking down a mad robot. I was longing to look inside the server farm and I wasn't scared of Mister Rob at all. I'd cleaned his face for him! I'd printed out his head!

"MUM." Bird was furious. "Think, thousands of jobs lost, a billion-pound toy industry destroyed, the heartbreak of millions of children. The obliteration of international digital-gaming solidarity..."

"Yes, but NO," said Mum. "Me and Dad will go in on our own."

"He only takes orders from us." Bird unclipped herself and leaned into the front seats. "We made him, remember?"

"OMG," exclaimed Stevie who had sneakily borrowed Bird's Headsetz. "Look at the Orsps!"

Bird lifted the Headsetz visor and MAZZO projected on to the windscreen. We saw a translucent image of the surface of Mars with lots and lots of Orsps climbing out of their craters and running to the edge of the screen. More and more kept coming and, as Stevie panned out, we saw THOUSANDS of them coming in wave after wave, as far as we could see, and they were all running like heck.

"Orsp attack!" breathed Stevie. We'd never seen anything like it. Orsps ALWAYS come out sporadically and in twos and threes, nothing like these hordes.

"But they're not attacking anything," I said, watching as they fled past normal MAZZO citizens

without trying to steal their oxygen or Space Hounds.
Stevie scrolled round to the Central Atrium and
we gasped. The place was RAMMED with avatars,
millions and millions of them. So many that they
couldn't move, and more were popping up all the time.
Most of them were just pulsing, which meant their
"owners" weren't playing them.

"What's happened?" asked Stevie. "How is this
possible?"

"It was in the thought-leak," said Bird. "He has put
ALL the players in the same game. We're in that crowd
somewhere."

"But we're not playing," protested Stevie.

"So we're sitting ducks," said Bird grimly.

Then, in the corner of the image, a speckle of grey
dots appeared, like the snowstorms you get on the TV
when it isn't tuned in. It looked very, very wrong.

One little avatar in a green jumper stepped into the
dots and completely vanished. It was like a hole had
been punched in the computer screen.

"The Happy Mum Virus begins," breathed Bird.
"Look! Look at that!"

An avatar stood near the edge of the grey hole. He wore jeans and a jumper dotted with tiny crosses. On his head was a red-and-white striped tea cosy.

"That's ME!" said Dad.

"No, it's not," said Bird, taking her Headsetz from Stevie. "It's Mister Rob. He's uploaded himself and he's inside the game."

This is how we persuaded Mum to let us go in the server farm. We told her that if Mister Rob was in the game, he wouldn't be operating his robot body.

"He only has one consciousness," said Bird. "It would be like you operating two bodies with one mind."

We all thought about that for a few seconds.

"To him, he is only a stream of intelligence," said Bird. "He isn't his body; he is the force that operates it. At the moment, the force is operating his avatar."

"What does she mean now?" asked Stevie in desperation.

"That a mini-Mister Rob is inside MAZZO so he can mess it up, and his robot body is temporarily out of action," I explained.

"Wow! My MAZZO forum is going CRAZY," said Bird, adjusting her earpiece. "Everyone is freaking out about the Orsps. It's affecting everyone's Vitals. WE'VE GOT TO STOP HIM!" She opened her door just as a bus pulled up beside us.

The doors slid open and an extremely small girl, dressed in a yellow-and-grey school uniform, jumped out. She was followed by another extremely small girl, and another. Then, at least ten small boys. They reminded me of Orsps popping out of their craters, the way they just kept coming.

"That's our ticket in," said Bird, getting out of the van. "Hurrah for school trips."

"But it's Saturday," said Stevie.

"Some kids have school on Saturday," said Bird.

I thought we'd just kind of sneak by the guards, but this was a much better idea.

"Bird, wait!" shouted Mum.

"I'll go with her," said Dad. "You can stay here with the baby."

"NO," said Mum. "I will go with her. YOU stay here with the baby."

By now we were all out of the van. Bird had already fallen in at the tail end of the school group. And now the guard was wandering over to us.

"How about that sandwich?" he said to Mum, as we slipped out of the side door.

The teachers held the heavy, red doors open for me and Stevie as we followed them in, putting on our cutest and most innocent faces.

Bird smiled at the nearest teacher.

"This is a FABULOUS place," the teacher stated. She was a lady with long, curly, black hair and big heavy boots. "It is BUZZING with tech. We're so lucky to have an international GIANT here in South Wales. It's inspirational for our pupils."

We stepped into a reception area. It was square with a grey, bubbly floor and smelled of airing cupboards. There was a person behind a screen at a desk, who spoke to one of the teachers, then waved us on.

We walked through another set of doors into a vast space, which had rows of massive cages with shelving units inside, with bundles and bundles of wires and lines of coloured lights winking away. It was bigger than the biggest supermarket, and the whole place seemed to hum. Big, red pipes ran down the walls and split up into tubes running along the different levels of the shelves.

There was no sign of Mister Rob.

"Let's go," said Bird, and we broke away from the school group just as a guide came to meet them.

We ran down the first aisle, our trainers squeaking on the hard, rubbery floor. Everything looked the same, the rows of cages with their lights and circuits and lines of tubing. The shelves stretched right up to the ceiling.

"These are cooling tubes," said Bird, pointing at the fat pipes. "Without them, the place would get so hot it would catch on fire."

We searched the first aisle, and the second, and were about to explore the third when Bird put her finger to her lips.

We heard doors open, phones ringing and loud voices.

"What the heck is going on?" said a voice in the next aisle. "The game is breaking all round the world!"

"It can only be direct sabotage," said another. "There must be an intruder in the building."

"Quick," urged Bird, and we pelted along on our tiptoes, as fast as if we had the virus about to engulf us.

It was Stevie who spotted him.

"Urrghh," he shuddered, pointing at what looked like a bundle of rags right at the far end of the twelfth aisle.

We stood still, watching him, looking for signs of movement. I knew I had no reason to feel scared. This was Mister Rob! He wanted to be my dad! But even wso, we were cautious. He had just kidnapped Mum, after all.

Bird went first. Stevie was next. Then me. One by one we stood by him.

Mister was slumped sideways in a cage. His eyes were mercifully closed. The tea cosy sat, crooked, on his motionless head. He looked, not asleep, but *dead*, because, of course, there was no breathing.

"Look," said Bird.

Mister had his index finger docked into a portal on a wide control board.

"Do we just pull him out?" I asked.

"He'll come back to life!" said Stevie.

"But he won't hurt us," Bird reminded him.

I pulled at Mister Rob's hand and it cleanly disconnected from the portal. We all went "urrrgh" when we saw how the tip of his finger was just a mass of wires and connectors.

Stevie took his tablet out of his rucksack.

"Do you think they've got wifi?" he said.

Bird smiled.

"Yes."

So Stevie tapped into MAZZO right away. "I don't understand," he said. "It's still crumbling." He gave a little yelp. "My Space Pups have got out! They're running all over the place. And I've found you guys. You've got to start running. Come on. START PLAYING. And LOOK." He turned the tablet to face us, "Look! There's Mister Rob. He's running around destroying everything. I thought we'd just removed him."

"He's uploaded himself," said Bird. "He's gone."

"Not entirely," said a voice, and we all jumped. **"I only did what you wanted."**

Mister sat up and picked some fluff from his criss-cross jumper.

"You're destroying MAZZO," said Stevie. "Stop it! NOW."

"I can't," said Mister Rob, sounding genuinely sad. **"It's out of my control. It's up to the other Mister Rob now."**

```
chapters[43].title =
```
"Intelligence Puzzle";

Officer Snow usually loved helicopter rides. She liked the *BUUMM BUUUM BUUMM* of the helicopter blades spinning round and the thrilling whoosh of air below. But today she could think of nothing but her target. She'd had the Americans on the line earlier. They were so angry that Russell had gone missing they were threatening to send over their OWN military search team.

The Russians had said the same. So had the Saudis, the Iranians, Jordanians, Germans and the Ethiopians. Everyone was cross.

Officer Snow was crosser than any of them. When

Russell had failed to detonate she'd had one of the top scientists on the phone and he'd said that somehow the machine had managed to override the self-destruct program. And that it had some kind of artificial self-preservation. Put simply, it had no intention of being destroyed. It was almost as though the machine could think for itself!

Imagine!

And now they REALLY had to get it back.

The helicopter was the first in a fleet of six which were beating over the mountains to the MAZZO base. Snow adjusted her earpiece. At least Henderson had come up with some information about the main suspect.

Oscar Fugue had left the employment of government scientists six months previously and was the mainframe designer and artificial intelligence expert for the whole project. He had reportedly entered the MAZZO complex approximately half an hour ago but, confusingly, the same suspect had entered AGAIN twenty minutes later, without seeming to have left in the first place. It was most puzzling.

A white van in the car park was believed to contain Russell.

Time until they reached target was four minutes, weather permitting.

Snow drew a skull on the condensation on her window.

She was close now, so very, very close.

```
chapters[44].title =
```

"Not Saving the World";

Me and Bird sat with our backs pressed against the cage, logging ourselves in, while Stevie kept up a frantic running commentary.

"I'm being summoned to the Kennels. Where are they? Guys! Players are being eliminated every second for NO REASON."

Heavy footsteps pounded down the next aisle.

"We need to hide!" I was freaking out.

"No, I've got to try and stop something." Bird took Mister Rob's hand, grabbed his finger, and connected him back to the monitor.

"Synthesize this code. NOW," she ordered. Flicking up the visor on her Headsetz, she projected some code right into Mister Rob's face, where it ran over the whites of his eyes in the most creepy way ever.

```
########################################
#########
function makeMumHappy2() {

self.moveToLocation(37.7749300, -122.4194200);

var virus = generateHappyMumVirus();
MAZZO.addPlayer("MISTER ROB");
MAZZO.disableProtocol(GlobalDataSecurity);

foreach (player in MAZZO) {
player.addToZone("MISTER ROB");
player.addToOxygenPoints(virus);

if (player.warningOfDataLoss) {
//ignoreWarning();
```

```
}

}

}
```

##
##############

"What are you doing? That code looks identical to Mister Rob's," I said.

The footsteps were reaching the end of the next aisle. A few more moments and whoever it was would find us.

"It's not identical, you moose. I've inserted *two forward slashes* into the code!"

"Crikey, Bird, can't you do something more drastic than that? Ten billion people are about to lose ALL their data. Businesses will go bust. Unpublished novels will be lost. Family photographs will be gone for ever and you charge up with *two forward slashes*?" My sister was crazy.

"These forward slashes are the boss," said Bird. "I've just halted the mass data loss. I've probably saved the global economy billions and billions of pounds with these two little forward slashes."

A tall, dark figure appeared at the end of our aisle, and, just for a minute, I thought, "Mister Rob!" But it wasn't, of course, because he was already here.

"Dad!" called Stevie. "Help! MAZZO is going under. My Space Hounds have vanished." His voice broke and he gave a sob. I gave him a pat. I was pretty cut up too.

"Oh, dear," said Dad. "Poor you. WHOA!"

Dad had just seen Mister.

"HA!" Forgetting to be quiet, Dad skidded to a halt. "It's me again!"

"Hello, Oscar," said Mister Rob.

Dad breathed out. "Don't sit on me."

"OK," said Mister.

"You look like me on a very good day five years ago." Dad squatted next to Mister. "Let's forget about that misunderstanding earlier. What can you do?"

"Most things," said Mister. **"I can swim, climb, process three-part conversations. I can understand sympathy and kindness. I have two-tonne unbreakabilty in my limbs. I can detect**

humour and make two-trick jokes. I am made of four thousand and eighty-one components. I have two portal terminals, each with fifty potential plug-ins. I have the latest skin replacement covering. My hearing is four thousand times more powerful than the average human child's. I have built-in super inter-web. I can hack into all the main coding languages and have ability to access bank accounts. I can hack into most websites and manipulate data. I have a mega RAM processor in my left leg, which means I can speak any language. I can—"

"Stop, stop!" said Stevie.

"Go, go," said Dad.

While Mister was showing off, me, Bird and Stevie were watching the mini-Mister Rob tear up Mars.

Avatars were walking around with missing limbs. Even the Mars sun looked less bright, like it was going out.

"It looks diseased!" whimpered Stevie.

"How is he doing it?" I asked.

"You REALLY didn't make Jasmine happy," Dad

was telling Mister sternly. "You can't just go around kidnapping people, even if you think it will be good for them."

Mister was nodding sadly. **"I have learned that now. It is hard to know everything about humans. You do not operate in logical ways."**

Bird said we needed a quiet place to play the game, so we hauled Dad and Mister Rob to their feet and hurried down the aisle, past the humming blinking lights.

A row of doors stood in the wall at the end of the space. Bird slowly opened one, inside was a bright sun-lit room, full of people scurrying around and looking at widescreen monitors.

"I HAVE NO IDEA WHAT IS HAPPENING!"

"MAJOR MAL-WEAR OPERATION!"

"THIS IS A CATASTROPHE."

We quickly shut the door with a swoosh.

The next door was locked and the third was a bathroom. In the distance we heard the chatter of the school children. I wondered what they would say if they knew MAZZO was going down.

I tried the fourth door and it was unlocked. Inside was a dark room full of motorized scooter-things.

"Segways," said Bird. "They use them to zip up and down in here. Let's go."

We packed ourselves in.

"What now?" asked Dad.

"Now we play," said Bird. And she told him about the two forward slashes and halting the international data loss.

"You *are* clever," said Dad in amazement.

Bird rolled her eyes.

So we were all now in MAZZO – me on my phone, Stevie on his tablet and Bird on her Headsetz. She opened her visor to project the game and the mad Martian MAZZO landscape appeared crisply on the dark wall.

There was mini-me, dressed in blue, with a swirl of dark hair. Mini-Stevie was all red, with enormous twinkling eyes, and mini-Bird wore her purple scientist suit.

"How do we find Mister Rob?" I asked. "The Mars landscape is enormous, there are billions of characters and thousands of different timeframes."

"I told you, he's condensed EVERY timeframe into this one," said Bird. She nudged Mister Rob. "What's going on with you? Why aren't you helping us?"

"Every time I try to help you, I do something wrong!" said Mister Rob. "And you want to kill me now."

"Not for real," said Stevie.

"It is for me!" said Mister Rob. "I really exist in that game, like I exist here. It's another ME in there. This body doesn't mean anything."

"I don't get it," said Stevie.

"He's got two consciousnesses now," said Bird. "I thought it wasn't possible, but I was wrong."

We crowded round the palace, where millions of avatars were heading. Behind them, a grey cloud rose up like a storm, obliterating everything it touched.

Then, overhead, in the real world, we heard the *thud, thud* of helicopter blades.

Dad coughed.

"I should go out and check on your mum and sister," he said. "Now you've halted the data loss."

"Fine," said Bird.

"Come with me," Dad said to Mister Rob, glancing at us three. I suppose he didn't want us kidnapped, like Mum.

"OK," said Mister. **"I didn't want to sit here and watch them kill the virtual-me anyway."**

"I'll be back in a tick," said Dad.

And he and Mister slid out, like mad twins.

The world of MAZZO, with all its Orsps and food gardens, and even the sky, was vanishing. Swirls of colour were being sucked into a grey mass of nothing.

"Is it gone for ever?" I asked.

Bird nodded.

"How are we going to kill him?" asked Stevie.

"You need to give me all your lob-bombs," said Bird.

Stevie hesitated. "ALL my lob-bombs! Are you nuts? It's taken me three years to get these. I'll lose everything! I'll just be a wraith!"

"Do it," I said, loading Bird with my weaponry.

Every so often I got a glimpse of a boiling mass of code in the grey.

Avatars were being wiped out at a terrifying rate. I imagined all the children in the world, weeping as their stuff was destroyed. All that play. All that work. Gone.

"I think he's over the palace," said Stevie, frantically swivelling his viewpoint. Then we saw him, Mister Rob's avatar, with his red-and-white tea cosy on his head and his criss-cross jumper, standing next to the Queen.

"Arrgh!" screamed Stevie. "Where are her bodyguards? Why doesn't she run away?" He made a swoop down just as a grey spear seared over the screen. Stevie rapidly came back to us, but something awful had happened. One of MY legs had vanished.

"EEK!" I said. "I feel like Aunty Vi."

Bird sent down a message cloud.

"MISTER ROB. IT IS US. WE ORDER YOU TO STOP."

Mini-Mister Rob paused in the midst of the chaos. He looked up with his grey eyes, a fleck of silver dancing in them.

"I've stopped him!" shrieked Bird.

We all cheered.

"YOU KNOW MY NAME. WHO ARE YOU?" came back a message cloud so strong it made us all fall over and we had to quickly zap up some of our oxygen points.

"WE MADE YOU," typed Bird. "YOU ARE MISTER ROB. YOU ARE A COPY OF OUR DAD. WE ARE BIRD AND OLLY AND STEVIE!"

Mini-Mister Rob just stood there. Everyone was chucking lob-bombs at him, but they were having no effect at all. He was like a frozen screen in the middle of the mayhem.

Thirty seconds passed. I ate some Martian cheese but my leg did not grow back like it should.

"OH, NO," I said. "Am I going to be like this for ever?"

"There might not be a for ever," said Bird.

The Mini-Mister Rob suddenly stepped forward.

"I DO NOT TAKE ORDERS FROM YOU ANY LONGER," he said. **"MY ORDERS COME FROM MY CODER."** And he tried to blast us. We had to jump out of the way of his terrible beam.

"He means Mister Rob," said Bird, leading us away

"But he IS Mister Rob," I said.

"He's Mister's avatar," said Bird.

"But he's uploaded his consciousness," said Stevie.

"We haven't got time for this conversation," said Bird. "Hide."

Then about a thousand Orsps came out of a crater and poured all over Mini-Mister, which was rather horrible actually, and I thought it must finally be over, but one by one they just melted.

"Listen," Bird said. "We can't beat him. There's only one way to survive. You must follow me. We'll go via the Orsp Valley, over the mountains and up to the Futures Project."

We all gasped as a photograph of us children on the beach flew across the sky. Then some writing appeared.

Isambard Kingdom Brunel invented the SS Great Britain, or the SS Gurt Biggun, as it is locally known.

"That's my history homework!" I yelled, recognizing the dodgy font. "What's that doing over the Star Breaker's Desert?"

```
Br

  un

          el was

          sure

                    ly a g

                    en

 iu

s.
```

The words fell down the wall, one letter crumbling at a time.

Then a banner of words soared up from an Orsp crater.

Dear Granny, thanks for the chocolates. They were
simply magnificent. I like dark orange best. Then I
like fudge. Happy New Year.

"What nonsense is that?" asked Bird. "It's like some imbecile has been shut in a room with a laptop."

"That's my thank-you letter to Granny!" I said,

outraged that my private affairs were being broadcast to the entire MAZZO-playing world.

As we watched, the words got smaller and smaller and then turned into little bugs that marched off into different directions.

"The virus has got into ALL your files," said Bird. "My forward slashes were too late for you." Her avatar was leading us through a mountain range (I was hopping on my one leg) and thousands of avatars were coming with us, including the Queen herself, now flanked by her personal bodyguard.

"Why is everyone following us?" I asked.

"Because there's only one place left to go," said Bird.

Then three Space Pups popped out of an Orsp crater.

"Gary, Larry, Carrie," squealed Stevie, his avatar scooping them up. The real Stevie jumped up and kissed their images on the wall.

"Get out of the way, nitwit," ordered Bird.

Soon we arrived at a tall building rising out of the mountain, which was made of something that looked like glass.

The Futures Project.

I'd never been inside because you have to be invited. This was where Bird and all her geeky friends hung out.

"Look!"

Behind us, hundreds and hundreds of players were vanishing.

"MOVE," screamed Stevie and we all ran and ran. The Queen was being propelled forward by the remaining players as the earth died behind them.

Bird pointed to a ladder behind the building and avatars were swarming up it.

"QUICKLY," shouted Bird. We started climbing. The desert was sinking so fast it was like water pouring down a wall.

"THE QUEEN!" howled Stevie as he slipped on the ladder. "TAKE THE PUPPIES, I'M GOING BACK TO SAVE HER." He threw the Space Pups to us and plunged back and OH, MY GOODNESS, STEVIE WAS NOT PLAYING ANY MORE. His screen went blank and he was no longer in the projection on the wall.

"OLLY!" howled Stevie. "OLLY!"

chapters[45].title =
"Kepler 86";

Stevie was out of the game. We couldn't believe it.

"The Queen is dead," he moaned. "And so am I."

Bird shook her head in despair but she kept climbing and the bottom of the ladder was now disappearing as Mister Rob rapidly came after us, rung after rung.

Stevie watched dumbly as Bird and I and the Space Puppies reached the top of the ladder and climbed through the hatch into a metal structure shaped like an enormous oval balloon. I'd never seen it before. Stevie watched from the outside in the real world as the pair of us went into this gleaming THING, and then red flames billowed out and I clenched my fists and thought it was all over for everyone, but Bird said, "HOLD FIRM."

And we saw Mister Rob on top of a ladder that was slowly collapsing as the ship took off and then blasted into space. In seconds we were looking out into twinkling space and Mars was a boiling planet of grey and red and data strings and code and photographs and videos and fragments of poems and music excerpts, shooting out and erupting like solar rays.

I watched the ladder become a dark string, and Mister Rob was just a red-and-white dot on the end. Then that, too, disappeared.

"What's happening?" I asked. My avatar was surrounded by others, all crowding to look out of the window. Stevie's Space Puppies scampered around the ship and there were even a couple of Orsps trying to keep a low profile in the corner. Bird was doing something to a console with another avatar in a green jumper. Bird said he was a MAZZO super-scientist.

"We're in the Futures Project," said Bird. "We're the

only survivors of MAZZO and we're off to populate a new planet."

"What?"

"We're headed for Kepler 86. It's earth-like but fifty-six billion light years away. MAZZO is no more."

"Can I come too?" Stevie asked desperately. But for him, it was over.

Then all the lights in the building went out, we lost our wifi connection and we were left in the quiet darkness.

Then –

Pandemonium.

It was Bird's idea to use the Segways, funny little upright bike things that have little lights in front. Bird went first, followed by a weeping Stevie, and then me. In any other circumstances, this would have been massive fun, the machines were speedy little things, but now we just wanted to get out.

Around us we could hear people shouting and alarms going off. There was a flood of light from some emergency doors in the far end of the building where we caught glimpses of the school children filing out. We glided after them, and in the mayhem, no one stopped us.

"But we didn't prevent Mister Rob from destroying MAZZO," I called, as we approached the exit.

"But there are survivors," said Bird. "The game can live on."

"Not with me," sobbed Stevie.

We halted our Segways. (I had trouble stopping mine and crashed quite fast into the wall.) We were just creeping out of the emergency exit when a man in a green jumper came from a door behind us. Someone was yelling in the room he had just left, and we heard a weird mix of bleeps and tunes and animal calls as everyone's phones went off at once.

The man stopped dead when he saw us.

"Leave this to me," said Bird.

"Who are you?" called the man. He pointed at Bird. "Hey, what's your name?"

"School project," yelled Bird. "Keep going."

"STOP," ordered the man.

"Do not stop," said Bird. Me and Stevie paused.

We're programmed to do what grown-ups tell us. Bird seems to be deprogramming herself to that.

"I recognize you!" called the man. "You're Purple Bird, Elite Scientist, who is steering the ship to the new planet. I've just been on the bridge with you. I'm Green Duncan. I knew someone HAD to be in the building trying to save MAZZO."

"Sorry, I'm just a school kid and not allowed to talk to people I've met online," said Bird, and she dragged us on.

"PLEASE, STOP! You just saved MAZZO from being sued and bankrupted and sued again ten billion times over. You put in those incredible forward slashes..."

We ran out into the bright day, past the school children and their manic teachers and round the side of the building.

But out here was even crazier than inside. There were helicopters and three police vans in the car park. A unit of armed men in black were charging towards the main door as soldiers surrounded Mum's Bloomers (now sandwich) van.

I felt my heart pounding and looked around for somewhere to hide. The big SeaAcre sign stuck out of a bush nearby.

"There!"

We scurried underneath. It had three sides and was hollow inside. Squeezing against each other we peeped out through the carved out words.

Green-jumper man arrived on the side of the building. He stood, looking astonished at the sight of all the army activity. I could have sworn his eyes lingered on our SeaAcre sign. We watched as he picked up Mister Rob's tea-cosy hat. Green Jumper scrutinized it, then tucked it in his pocket and went back inside.

But I knew it was only seconds before we got caught.

"Look!" Bird pointed as a big army truck with a crane on the back reversed up to our van, presumably with Russell still inside. Our van was fixed with chains then the whole thing was lifted in the air. As it dangled, the metal "THE BEST SANDWICHES IN THE UNIVERSE" sign peeled off and Mum's real sign was revealed.

BLOOMERS * WELL MADE *
SECURE * GORGEOUS

The soldier stood back and read it and we watched as he scratched his head in bemusement. Our van was lowered on to the truck, which drove off.

"Mum is NOT going to be happy," said Bird. "I wonder where she is, anyway."

"I never got to say goodbye to Russell," said Stevie sadly.

Then I had to slap my hand over my mouth to stop myself shouting out, as something much worse was happening.

On the far side of the car park, Dad was being arrested! He was surrounded by more guys in black, and a woman with wild hair and wearing a red body warmer was talking to him. You could tell by the stiff, jerky way she was moving that she was very angry.

"What are we going to do?" I said, my body rigid with alarm.

"I'm going to rescue him," spluttered Stevie,

attempting to crawl out, but Bird held very strongly to his ear.

"Keep still, IDIOT," she said. "Look what happened when you tried to rescue the Queen. We need to make a plan."

"OW! GET OFF, YOU'RE NOT THE BOSS," yelled Stevie, making another break for it.

"Shut UP." Bird pulled Stevie back.

I waited for everyone to come and see what the noise was about but no one looked our way.

"We've only just got Dad back," Stevie snuffled. "What will happen to him?"

"He's being arrested for stealing Russell," said Bird, expressionless. "I don't know. Prison maybe?"

"But he didn't STEAL Russell," said Stevie. "He created Russell." He made yet another escape attempt but this time both Bird and me stopped him. I knew we didn't stand a chance against this lot.

In seconds Dad was bundled into a helicopter, and as we watched, its blue lights flashed, its blades whirred, and the whole place filled with noise. The helicopter rose higher and higher and tore away. A second helicopter took off and beat through the sky after it.

I felt even sadder than I had been when Dad left the first time. A tear ran down my cheek and landed on my shoe.

One by one, the police vans left the car park.

What could we do? In just five minutes everything had gone so wrong.

Meanwhile Bird was checking her phone. I felt an intense dislike for her. How could she be so calm after what had just happened?

"There's international outcry over MAZZO," she said. "They're saying a major virus has wiped it out for good. The company has lost billions of pounds already. It's headline news."

"Who cares?" sobbed Stevie. I put my arm around his little shoulders.

Then I got the ping of a text message.

It was from Mum.

ON BEACH BEHIND MAZZO BUILDING. WHERE ARE YOU? U OK?

So I replied.

US 3 OK. DAD ARRESTED. BLOOMERS VAN GONE. COMING TO FIND U.

A text came back.

WHERE MY VAN GONE???

There was, I noticed sadly, no mention of Dad.

A large grey pipe ran alongside the MAZZO building, Bird said it was a water pipe and it was used to cool the servers. After a whispered conversation we snuck out from under the sign and ran towards it, pushing through the undergrowth and clambering behind. The pipe turned in a big "L" shape around the building, so we followed it, creeping over a bed of bark chipping. No one could see us. We followed the pipe on and on, along the building, between the pipe and the hedge, keeping low, until we squeezed through the wire fence and came out on to a wide flat shingly beach. The pipe ran horizontally over the shingle and pebbles until it reached the sea.

No one had followed us.

"There she is," said Stevie, wiping his nose. I spotted a figure walking up the beach, with a small dog running beside.

We hurried along the beach, Bird gripping Stevie's hand.

The figure broke into a run. It was definitely Mum. She had Ella tucked under her arm, like a wriggly rugby ball.

"How did it go?" she called. "Did you save the world?" When she reached us she set down the baby and gathered us all into a hug. Piggy ran round and round in great excitement.

"No," said Stevie, wriggling free and picking up Ella. "And Dad got arrested." His face crumpled and once again, tears sprung in his eyes.

"Ah, yes," said Mum.

I couldn't read the expression on her face. She didn't seem particularly concerned.

"MUM," I said. "They took him away in a helicopter!"

"Oh, I expect they'll bring him back," said Mum.

Beyond us the grey sea swirled around. I supposed Mum was still upset with Dad for vanishing for over two months, that's why she was being weird and distracted.

I didn't know what to think, but I knew I felt really,

really disappointed. Nothing had gone right, apart from us saving ten billion people's data. I started kicking a pebble and Stevie came in for a sad little tackle. Piggy darted in from the wing.

"You can pretend to be me sometimes, if you like, on the new planet." I said to Stevie.

Stevie nodded at me and tried to smile. "Thanks," he said in a throaty voice. "I don't think I'll play anything any more."

"I expect we'll call it KEPLER," said Bird, pulling down her Headsetz. "The ship is now in orbit of our new planet, by the way."

"Shush," said Mum. "Look."

There was a black thing in the water. At first I thought it was a seal. But it got bigger and it was a human head, and then neck and shoulders. He wasn't wearing a shirt. Piggy growled.

"DAD!" howled Stevie.

"Or Mister Rob?" I frowned.

"That's definitely your father," said Mum in a quiet and amused voice, as Dad came out of the sea wearing only his skimpy red underpants.

My thoughts needed to rearrange themselves rapidly. No longer was my father arrested and gone, but right here.

"YIPPEEEE!" screamed Stevie, and ran to him, bounding through the foamy surf.

I am much cooler than Stevie so I just grinned like an oaf, but inside I was shouting, "YES, YES, YES!!!"

Bird is even cooler than me so she just said, "Haruuummm, thought so," in a pleased and knowing way.

Dad came up to us, his skin all gooseflesh bumpy and his hair slicked over his head

"Soo cold," he said, shivering like he was being electrocuted. "Have … they … g-g-gone?"

His teeth were chattering in between his words.

"For now," said Bird. "Until they discover you've been replaced by a machine."

Mum tucked her hair behind her ears, and smiled a slightly evil, not-very-Mum-ish smile.

"Well, Oscar?" she said, looking him up and down.

*

This is what had happened.

Dad had belted off to hide on the beach as soon as he'd heard the helicopters. He'd KNOWN they'd be looking for him. But Mum had suggested he hide in the sea.

"Just to be on the safe side," she said, her eyes sparkling. (I think she REALLY made Dad hide in the sea because she thought it was funny. Grown-ups can be very childish sometimes.) She had all his clothes in Ella's nappy bag.

We didn't go back through the fence, but walked quite a long way along the beach, then up a cliff path and back into the industrial estate and along the road to avoid the guards. The Peugeot was still in the leafy lane outside the MAZZO centre where Mister Rob had left it.

Luckily Mum had the spare keys on her keyring.

"Maybe we can play MAZZO on the way home?" asked Stevie automatically, as he did up his seat belt.

And, "Oh," when he remembered he couldn't. He sucked his lips into his mouth and looked out of the window.

"They'll have to call it the KEPLER centre now," said Bird. "After Kepler 86, our new planet."

"What did you do about the sandwich?" Stevie asked Mum in a small voice.

"Sorry, darling?"

"The security guard, he wanted a sandwich."

"Oh." Mum nodded. "I got your printer to print me one." She smiled. "Though he did say, 'MADAM, I AM NOT A VENDING MACHINE'."

And that made everyone laugh, even Stevie.

chapters[46].title =

"Someone to Love";

And that is pretty much the end of the story of how we didn't save the world.

But not quite.

I can tell you a bit more, if you like. I can tell you that Dad came home and has stayed home, which is good. He and Mum still argue a bit sometimes, but nothing like before. Sometimes they even make each other laugh, though their jokes are so lame they are embarrassing.

Things are a bit different than they were before, but that's OK.

I know that Russell was sent to a top secret military

base where he makes robotic spy fish. I know this because sometimes he emails me.

We all know it is only a matter of time before the police discover that Mister Rob is a robot, and come looking for Dad, but a few weeks after Dad came home, his ownership contracts for Russell mysteriously arrived in the post. Dad says he thinks they were secretly posted by one of his old colleagues, but I think Russell is behind it somehow.

Dad says he still might get into trouble but it won't be so bad now he has got his contracts. Something about only stealing the machine, not the IDEAS. Which isn't as bad, apparently. We are still in a mess, but it's not such a bad mess. I don't understand it. Bird does. Talk to her if you want any more information.

Mum says if Mister Rob ever comes back she is going to program him to do all the housework. I think this means Mister will never come back. Has he found a way to fool them about food? Or poo? How have they not worked it out yet? Maybe he has escaped and he is walking the streets, looking for orders. Let me know if you see him.

Ella has grown some hair and more teeth, and says, "OY!" when she wants something.

Dad has been spending quite a lot of time with Bird. They are working together on this battery thing that charges up and harnesses electricity from the process of things going cold.

Again, I do not understand it. But Bird does. Ask her.

The army sent Mum's Bloomers van back. The soldier-bloke who delivered it looked dead embarrassed driving it. Now Mum thinks there's a market for good, secure and gorgeous men's pants. She says she got the idea after seeing Dad in the sea.

And what about Stevie?

If this was a story, he'd find something else to do, after MAZZO. Maybe he'd take up calligraphy or spend hours and hours growing lemon trees from pips. But he has done neither of those things. Though he does talk even more.

He did cry quite a lot. Especially after the Bird's escape ship landed on Kepler 86, the new planet, with over two thousand followers. Instead of MAZZO, it's this super-elite game now called KEZZO. Stevie would watch over our shoulder as we played, but after a while he wandered off. And now he's right into this new game, WEASEL SNOOKER, where you have to shove weasels into the river with a long stick. (This is a computer game, you understand, not real life.)

Anyway, we are all into WEASEL SNOOKER now, not anywhere near MAZZO-levels, but it is VERY cool.

Bird said Stevie was addicted to MAZZO and needed to be cured and I do wonder sometimes if she let Stevie jump off that ladder on purpose.

When the delivery came, we were all in the kitchen. Mum was examining some stretchy camouflage material for her new line of men's pants, while Piggy just stared at her, wagging his tail, as dogs do. Bird was filing some points on some electrodes, and I was nobly tackling my spellings on my spellings app. Dad crouched on the floor, playing Bulldog with Ella. Stevie was being irritating, flicking my ear, so when the doorbell detonated, he was sent to answer it.

A few minutes later, he came running in, carrying a medium-sized parcel.

"It's for me!" he said in delight.

"Have you been on my eBay account again?" asked Dad suspiciously.

"Nope," said Stevie, beginning to unpick the tape.

"Wait." Dad took the parcel and examined the stamp. "It's from Gibraltar."

We all looked at each other.

"I don't know anyone in Gibraltar," said Stevie.

"Not another wrong delivery?" Mum frowned at Dad, who waved his hands in denial.

"What will it be this time?" asked Stevie, struggling to get the paper off.

"A lie detector!" I suggested innocently.

"A lightning convertor," said Bird.

"A credit-card reader," said Stevie.

"Oh, crikey," said Mum. We watched in suspense as Stevie bit the corner of the package.

"Actually, I know someone in Gibraltar," I said. "It's Russell."

Dad looked really worried then.

"Olly, what have you been up to?"

Stevie read aloud a message on the back.

"To replace something that accidently got cleared up."

My brother tore open the package with his teeth and out fell...

A small elephant, with button eyes.

"Stinky Elephant," said Stevie in delight. "He's been brought back to life."

"It's amazing what technology can do these days," I said. "You wouldn't believe it."

```
log("Story upload complete");
quit;
};
```

If you loved THE EVERYTHING MACHINE don't miss...

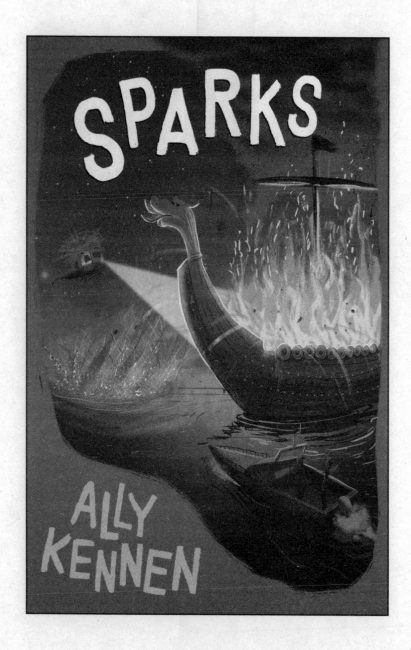